Kaleidoscope

Level C

Columbus, Ohio

Acknowledgments

Grateful acknowledgment is given to the following publishers and copyright owners for permissions granted to reprint selections from their publications. All possible care has been taken to trace ownership and secure permission for each selection included. In case of any errors or omissions, the Publisher will be pleased to make suitable acknowledgments in future editions.

"A Daring Escape" adapted from "Ellen Craft" from PROFILES OF NEGRO WOMANHOOD by Sylvia G.L. Dannett. Used by permission. GOOD LEMONADE by Frank Asch. Copyright © 1976 by Frank Asch. Used by permission of Franklin Watts, a division of Scholastic Library Publishing. "A Job for Ole Swenson" From JACK AND JILL, copyright © 1986 by Curtis Publishing Co. Used by permission of Children's Better Heath Institute, Benjamin Franklin Literary & Medical Society, Inc., Indianapolis, Indiana. "The Floating Market" from STREET MARKETS AROUND THE WORLD by Cecil Lubell and illustrated by Winifred Lubell. Used by permission of Winifred Lubell. "The First Napkins" from THE SOUP STONE by Maria Leach. COPYRIGHT 1954 BY FUNK & WAGNALLS COMPANY. Used by permission of HarperCollins Publishers. "The Secret of Room 5" adapted from THE STORY OF THOMAS ALVA EDISON, INVENTOR by Margaret Davidson. Copyright © 1964 by Margaret Davidson. Reprinted by permission of Scholastic Inc. "The First Foghorn" by Lucy Bowdler, copyright © 1953, renewed 1981 by Random House, Inc., from STORY PARADE. Used by permission of Golden Books, an imprint of Random House Children's Books, a division of Random House, Inc. "Nine-Day Nightmare" by Jacques Verdol from COIN LECTURE. Used by permission. "Emperors of the Ice" by Rona Lee Kleiman for RANGER RICK MAGAZINE. Used by permission. "How Lisa Learns to Talk" by Edna S. Levine from LISA AND HER SOUNDLESS WORLD. Used by permission. "The Horse Who Could Count" by Helen Kay from "How Smart Are Animals?" Used by permission. "Can Ants Communicate?" by Dorothy Van Woerkom from THE MAN WHO THOUGHT ANTS COULD TALK. Used by permission. "The Cave Paintings" by Theresa Barlett. From CITY SIDEWALKS (The Bank Street Readers, Grade 3) © 1966. Reproduced by permission of The McGraw-Hill Companies. "The Penobscot Hero" from KWI-NA EAGLE AND OTHER INDIAN TALES by M.A. Jagendorf. Used by permission. "How the Buffalo Lost a War" from STIFF EARS: ANIMAL FOLKTALES OF THE NORTH AMERICAN INDIAN by Alex Whitney, copyright © 1974 by Alex Whitney. Used by permission of Random House Children's Books, a division of Random House, Inc.

Photo Credits

22-23, ©Bettmann/Corbis; **24,** ©AP Wide World Photos; **25,** ©Hulton/Archive; **58,** ©Spencer Grant/PhotoEdit; **59,** ©Alan Oddie/PhotoEdit; **60,** ©Keren Su/Corbis; **61,** ©SuperStock; **62,** ©Kevin R. Morris/Corbis; **63,** ©James Marshall/Corbis; **70-71,** ©Bettmann/Corbis; **72,** ©Schenectady Museum; Hall of Electrical History Foundation/Corbis; **73 - 82,** ©Bettmann/Corbis; **83,** ©Corbis; **84,** (l) ©Spencer Grant/PhotoEdit, (tr) ©Morton & White, (br) ©Richard Hutchings/PhotoEdit; **85,** ©British Museum, London/Bridgeman Art Library, London/SuperStock; **87,** (tl) ©David Young-Wolff/PhotoEdit, (tr) ©Ralph A. Clevenger/Corbis; **88-89,** ©Tony Freeman/PhotoEdit; **96,** ©SuperStock; **97,** ©Neil Rabinowitz/Corbis; **122,** ©David Fritts/Animals Animals/Earth Scenes; **123-124,** ©Johnny Johnson/Animals Animals; **125,** ©G. Robertson/Photo Researchers, Inc.; **126,** ©Tim Davis/Photo Researchers, Inc.; **127,** ©G.L. Kooyman/Animals Animals; **156,** ©Bridgeman Art Library; **157-161,** ©Ronald Sheridan/Ancient Art & Architecture; **176-181,** (bkgd) ©Richard A. Cooke/Corbis; **177-181,** ©Christie's Images; **186,** ©John Neubauer/PhotoEdit; **187,** ©Susan Van Etten/PhotoEdit; **188,** ©SuperStock; **189,** ©Danny Lehman/Corbis.

www.sra4kids.com

Copyright © 2003 by SRA/McGraw-Hill.

All rights reserved. Except as permitted under the United States Copyright Act, no part of this publication may be reproduced or distributed in any form or by any means, or stored in a database or retrieval system, without the prior written permission of the publisher, unless otherwise indicated.

Send all inquiries to:
SRA/McGraw-Hill
8787 Orion Place
Columbus, OH 43240-4027

Printed in the United States of America.

ISBN 0-07-584125-8

4 5 6 7 8 9 RRC 07 06 05

Unit Themes

UNIT **1** **Risks and Consequences**

UNIT **2** **Dreams to Jobs**

UNIT **3** **What an Idea!**

UNIT **4** **Surviving**

UNIT **5** **Communication**

UNIT **6** **Native Americans**

Table of Contents

UNIT 1 Risks and Consequences

The Hound and the Fox 2
by Sharon Fear
illustrated by Joe Boddy

Spring Concert 6
by Gwen Sebring
illustrated by Linda Pierce

Vote for Tat 12
by Joe Gordon
illustrated by Tom Barrett

The Talk-Too-Much Tortoise 16
retold by Bonita DelRey
illustrated by Lane Yerkes

Rosa Parks Makes History 22
by Duncan Searl

A Daring Escape 26
by Sylvia G.L. Dannett
illustrated by Doris Ettlinger

Reading Reflections .32

Table of Contents

UNIT 2 Dreams to Jobs

Good Lemonade 34
by Frank Asch
illustrated by Len Epstein

A Job for Ole Svenson 38
by Paul Tulien
illustrated by Len Epstein

Wee Willie Goes Walking 44
by Carla Benedict
illustrated by Dave Blanchette

Tracy's First Job 48
by Westley Donaldson
illustrated by Deborah White

From Making Music to Making Food: Dreams That Change 52
by Joyce Mallery
illustrated by Barbara Kiwak

The Floating Market 58
by Winifred and Cecil Lubell

Reading Reflections 64

Table of Contents

UNIT 3 What an Idea!

The First Napkins .66
by Maria Leach
illustrated by Pat Morrison

The Secret of Room 5 70
by Margaret Davidson

And Away We Go! 76
by Ann Poole
illustrated by Brock Nicol

Where Do We Get All That Paper? 84
by Elsie Sea
illustrated by Alexander Farquharson

The First Foghorn .90
by Lucy Bowdler
illustrated by Alexander Farquharson

What's In a Name? .98
by Alex Petrovic
illustrated by Gary Torrisi

Reading Reflections 102

Table of Contents

UNIT 4 Surviving

Nine-Day Nightmare 104
 by Jacques Verdol
 illustrated by Yvonne Gilbert

Strong in the Saddle 110
 by Ann Murray
 illustrated by Linda Pierce

Water Crushes Steel 114
 by Nick Ramirez
 illustrated by Pat Paris

The Rooster and the Fox 118
 Aesop's fable retold by Alan Samuels
 illustrated by Judith Moffatt

Emperors of the Ice 122
 by Rona Lee Kleiman

Dolphin Rescue 128
 based on a true story and retold by Rebecca Brandenberg
 illustrated by Joe Boddy

Reading Reflections .134

Table of Contents

UNIT 5 Communication

How Lisa Learns to Talk 136
by Edna S. Levine
illustrated by Yemi

Can Windmills Talk? 142
by Allan Walldren
illustrated by Barbara Kiwak

The Horse Who Could Count 148
by Helen Kay
illustrated by Janice Skivington

Can Ants Communicate? 152
by Dorothy Van Woerkam
illustrated by Dave Blanchette

The Cave Paintings 156
by Theresa Bartlett

Haiku: Fun to Read, Fun to Write 162
by Laura Joseph
illustrated by Beatriz Rodriguez

Reading Reflections 168

Table of Contents

UNIT 6 Native Americans

The Penobscot Hero 170
*a Native American folktale retold by Martin Highbanks
illustrated by Fabricio Vanden Broeck*

Pearl Sunrise 176
by Nancy J. Nielsen

Sequoya's New Alphabet 182
*by Rob Howell
illustrated by Fabricio Vanden Broeck*

The Aztecs 186
by Walter Dubois

Kiana's Discovery 190
*by Sheri Cooper Sinykin
illustrated by Deborah White*

How the Buffalo Lost a War 194
*a Pawnee legend retold by Alex Whitney
illustrated by Dave Blanchette*

Reading Reflections 200
Glossary 202

The Hound and the Fox

by Sharon Fear
illustrated by Joe Boddy

There was once a big hound that hunted a fox. He hunted him every day. He chased him for weeks. But he never could catch that fast old fox.

So the hound thought of a way to trick the fox. One day when the fox was out, the hound went to the fox's den. He dug a deep pit just in front of it. He covered the pit with twigs and then put straw and dirt over them. On top of this he laid a feast. There were wild grapes, a fat hen, and eggs. And then the hound went away to wait.

The fox soon came back. He was amazed. There was a wonderful meal in his doorway! But he was a smart fox. He sat down a little way from the den and thought:

This food didn't come here by accident. Someone must have brought it. But a friend would have brought it when I was at home. I think I'd better hide for a while.

So the fox ran away to a safe place.

Soon after that, a hungry leopard came by. He saw the good food and rushed toward it. As soon as he stepped on the twigs and straw, they gave way, and he fell into the pit.

The hound, hiding nearby, heard the crash. He quickly ran to the pit and jumped in, thinking he'd caught the fox at last. Instead, he met an angry leopard.

And what was supposed to happen to the fox that day happened to the hound instead. He was gobbled up in three big bites!

Spring Concert

by Gwen Sebring
illustrated by Linda Pierce

Brianna and Vernon were going to sing a song together at the spring concert. They had practiced hard for weeks, but Vernon was nervous.

The day before the concert Vernon told Mr. Barnes, the music teacher, that he did not think he could perform.

"Let me ask you a few questions," Mr. Barnes said. "Do you feel as if you know the song?"

"Yes, I have it memorized," Vernon said.

Then Mr. Barnes asked, "Do you like to sing?"

"Very much," replied Vernon.

"Are you nervous about singing in front of other people?" Mr. Barnes said, going on with his questions.

"Well, maybe a little," Vernon admitted.

Then Mr. Barnes said, "Everybody gets a little nervous performing in public, especially the first time. Just go up there and sing it like you do in practice."

"Thanks, Mr. Barnes. I'll try," Vernon answered.

The next night Vernon was still nervous as he prepared for the concert. He said to Brianna, "What if I don't start singing at the right time? What if I forget the words? What if . . ."

"I know what you mean," said Brianna. "I'm nervous, too. But we can't back out now."

Just then Vernon heard Mr. Barnes introduce them to the audience. Brianna smiled at Vernon and started to walk on stage. With a gulp, Vernon followed her. The audience grew quiet as the piano started to play. "Just sing it like you do in practice," Vernon told himself. When the time came for Vernon's part, he began to sing. Before he knew it, the song was over, and the audience was smiling and applauding.

Bowing, Vernon looked into the audience and spotted his parents. He could tell by their smiles that they were very proud of him. Vernon also felt proud of himself.

"It was hard to get up on stage," he told Mr. Barnes the next day. "But it sure was worth it!"

Vote for Tat

by Joe Gordon
illustrated by Tom Barrett

At the end of the week, Tat's class would vote for class president. Tat was running for president even though he had tried last year and lost. He knew he could do a good job. His task was to convince the rest of his classmates. That would take a bit of work.

To begin his campaign, Tat spent three hours making a poster. It showed his picture and a list of promises that he would keep if elected. Tat got permission first thing Monday morning to put the poster near the door of his classroom. It was exactly where the students would see it each time they left the room.

Next, Tat made a campaign shirt out of one of his father's old T-shirts. He painted "Vote for Tat" on it. All day Tuesday he wore the shirt.

The next day Tat used his whole recess to talk to every student from his class. He told them why he would make a good president. Then Tat asked for their votes on Friday.

He spent all of Thursday evening writing a speech for election day. After two tries, Tat had a speech that he liked. Tat forgot part of his speech when he practiced it in front of Lin, his parents, and his stuffed animals. He was so worried that he would forget the speech the next day that he practiced it two more times. When he finished, his family congratulated him on a fine speech.

On Friday morning, Tat felt a little nervous as he dressed for school. He put on his favorite shirt, his lucky socks, and a new pair of pants with no holes in the knee. "Well, what do you think, Lin?" Tat said.

"You look like a winner to me," Lin replied. "Good luck today."

"Thanks," Tat said as he left for school.

Tat's speech had gone well, but he held his breath as the name of the new president was read. It took Tat a minute to realize that his hard work had finally paid off. He had won!

The Talk-Too-Much Tortoise

(A folktale from India)

Retold by Bonita DelRey
illustrated by Lane Yerkes

A tortoise made his home near a peaceful pond in the Himalaya Mountains. He was young, handsome in a wrinkled sort of way, and friendly. He was not at all like his cousin, the snapping turtle. The tortoise, however, had only one fault. He liked to talk a lot. In fact, he talked too much. He started most conversations with the phrase, "Let me tell you about . . . ."

One day, two brown geese came to the pond. They were searching for food. The tortoise began to talk to them as soon as they landed on the water.

Soon, the geese and the tortoise became great friends.

One day, the geese said, "We have a fine home on Mount Beautiful. Will you come and live with us, Friend Tortoise?"

The tortoise frowned. "I would like to go with you. I am an orphan and have no family. But how can I, a tortoise, get to your home?"

"We have already thought of that," said the geese. "All you need to do is keep from talking and don't wriggle. Do you think you can do that?"

"Of course I can do that!" the tortoise told them.

The geese found a sturdy stick. "It is a good thing that you are a tortoise and not an elephant," they said. Then they told the tortoise to clutch the stick with his mouth and reminded him not to wriggle. With their strong bills, each bird took hold of an end of the stick. The geese rose into the air and flew swiftly toward their home.

As they flew, they passed over a village and a palace. Some children saw the geese carrying the tortoise.

"Look! Look! Two geese are carrying a tortoise on a stick!" they shouted excitedly.

Their cries upset the tortoise. He wanted to call back to them. "Let me tell you about my friends. They have invited me to their home. They offered to carry me there."

As he opened his mouth to speak, he let go of the stick. The tortoise fell with great force. He landed in the palace courtyard, and that was the end of the tortoise.

Villagers ran into the courtyard to see the wreck. "A tortoise has fallen from the sky!" they shouted.

Everyone in the palace hurried to see what the excitement was about. The king himself came. So did the king's teacher.

The king turned to the wise man. "Teacher! What made this tortoise fall here?"

Now the wise man knew that the king himself talked a lot. Often no one could get a word in when the king talked. The wise man said, "My King, the tortoise talked too much, and it killed him."

The king looked at the wise man in amazement. "How could talking too much kill him?"

The wise man bowed and answered, "All he had to do was clutch the stick. But he just had to talk. When he opened his mouth, he let go of the stick. That was the end of him, my King."

From that day onward, the king always spoke thoughtfully and listened carefully.

Rosa Parks Makes History

by Duncan Searl

Rosa Parks Is Arrested

On December 1, 1955, Rosa Parks boarded a bus for home. Little did she know that her ride would go down in history.

At the next stop, some white riders boarded. One man had to stand. "Hey!" the bus driver yelled to Rosa. "Give this man your seat!" On the buses of Montgomery, Alabama, white riders got seats first.

Rosa did not budge.

"Make it light on yourself. Just give him your seat," the driver urged.

Rosa Parks

Inside a segregated bus

The driver's yell did not disturb Rosa. She stayed put. Giving in wouldn't "make it light" for her. The more African Americans gave in, the worse they were treated.

"I'll have you arrested," the driver warned.

Imagine his surprise at her answer.

"You may do that," Rosa replied.

At the next stop, two policemen zipped Rosa off to the city jail.

African Americans Protest

News of the arrest spread. African Americans got angry. They had had enough of segregation. Lawyers persuaded Rosa to become a test case. They wanted to prove that bus segregation was illegal. They would go all the way to the Supreme Court.

African Americans boycotted the buses. They formed carpools. They took cabs. They rode bikes. They walked. They did not ride the buses. A young minister in Montgomery led the protest. His name was Martin Luther King, Jr.

Dr. Martin Luther King, Jr.

Without African American riders, the bus company lost money. So did businessmen along the bus routes. They tried to stop the boycott. African Americans stood firm. They did not ride the buses.

Segregated Buses are Declared Illegal

After a year, news came from Washington. The Supreme Court agreed with Rosa that segregated buses were illegal. All citizens have the right to ride the buses.

The rest is history. The Civil Rights Movement had begun. Rosa Parks' case was the origin of it all!

The Civil Rights Movement had begun.

A Daring Escape

by Sylvia G.L. Dannett
illustrated by Doris Ettlinger

It was 1848. A coach stopped in front of the best hotel in Charleston, South Carolina. A man from the hotel came out to meet his guests.

An African-American servant opened the coach door. In the coach sat the servant's master, a young white man. He wore green glasses and was well dressed. He appeared to be a rich young planter. But it seemed he had been hurt. One arm was bandaged. Another bandage covered part of his face and head.

The young man presented himself. He was William Johnson, he said. He had had an accident while traveling. It had been a hazardous trip. Johnson's servant and the hotel man helped him inside.

At the hotel desk, there was a book to sign. But his guest could not sign it. His arm was hurt. "That's all right," said the hotel man. "I'll put your name in the book. It would be an honor to help you."

Johnson's servant helped him to his room. The door closed behind them. There, William Johnson took off the bandages. The dark glasses came off, too. The "young planter" was really Ellen Craft, an African-American woman! She was escaping from slavery in Georgia. Her "servant" was really her husband, William Craft. They were on their way to the North. In the North, there was no slavery. They would be free there.

It was dangerous to go north. Only brave people tried it. A coward would never take such a risk.

Slaves could not travel unless their owners allowed it. The Crafts had had to plan their escape very carefully. There would be no room for error. They also had to be good actors.

Ellen's skin was quite light. People had often thought that she was white. For their escape, she would cut her hair short and dress as a man. She would pretend to be a white slave owner. William would act as her slave. Then no one would stop them.

But Ellen could not read or write. What if someone asked her to write her name? She would pretend that her arm was hurt! She'd bandage it. Then no one would expect her to write. Another bandage on her face and head would help keep people from seeing who she was. It was a daring plan. Ellen and William were afraid. But they wanted to be free.

They began to buy pieces of clothing they would need. They kept these hidden. Ellen had to make the trousers she would wear. She did it secretly. William found a pair of dark glasses for Ellen. At last they were ready. Nothing could make them quit.

They started their trip by train. Ellen looked around the train car. Oh, no! There was Mr. Cray, a friend of her master! Surely, he would see her. Mr. Cray looked straight at Ellen. But he did not know who she was.

There were many such moments. There was much to fear. But at last they reached Boston. They were free!

UNIT 1

Reading Reflections

These questions can help you think about the stories you just read. After you write your responses, discuss them with a partner.

Focus on the Characters

- Compare and contrast the king and the tortoise in "The Talk-Too-Much Tortoise."
- Vernon practiced his song often in "Spring Concert." As a result, he did not give up and the concert went smoothly. Name another story where a character kept trying and reached his or her goal.
- What personal qualities did Ellen and William Craft have in "A Daring Escape" that helped make their escape successful?

Focus on the Stories

- How did Rosa Parks' one small act of defiance on a bus lead to bigger results?
- In "Vote for Tat," Tat devised a plan to help his campaign for class president. Name another story where planning ahead was the key to success.
- What problems did Ellen and William Craft have to plan for as they prepared for their escape in "A Daring Escape"?

Risks and Consequences

Focus on the Theme

- "Rosa Parks Makes History" is a selection that tells about the start of the Civil Rights Movement. Name another selection in this unit that tells about the risks African Americans faced in their struggle for freedom in America.
- At the end of "Spring Concert" Vernon says "It was hard to get up on stage but it sure was worth it!" Name other stories in this unit where the end result was worth the risks.
- Which story in this unit do you think had the greatest risks for the characters? Explain your choice.

Good Lemonade

by Frank Asch
illustrated by Len Epstein

One summer, Frank wanted to make some money. He wanted to make a lot of money.

"I'll make some lemonade," he thought. "Then I'll build a stand. I can sell it there."

Frank did just that. He spent the next day constructing the stand. On the first day he sold lemonade, things went well. Frank sold a lot of cups of lemonade, but by the next day the word was out.

"We don't like Frank's lemonade," his friends said. "It tastes terrible." None of them would buy it. All that Frank sold was one cup. That was to his little brother.

"A lemonade stand is a good idea," said Frank's friend Ana. "All you need now is some good lemonade."

"That's not it," said Frank. "What I need are some good signs." So he started to make some.

The signs said: *We love Frank's lemonade. Buy from Frank. Frank's lemonade is great!*

Frank hung the signs up by his stand. Then he sat back and waited for the money to roll in. But it was no good. All he sold was one cup. That was to his little brother. Frank was disappointed.

The next day Frank had another plan. He painted his stand. He decorated his paper cups. He offered a prize with each cup. But all he sold was one cup. That was to his little brother.

Next, Frank dressed up as "Mr. Happy Lemon" and jumped into a big pail of lemonade. All he sold was one cup. That was to his little brother. Unbelievable!

By this time Frank had run out of new ideas. Then he saw a lot of children coming down the street. They all went into his neighbor Ana's yard. Frank got up and followed them.

There in Ana's yard Frank saw another lemonade stand. His friends were buying Ana's lemonade!

"What is your secret?" asked Frank.

"Good lemonade!" answered Ana.

"I'll try anything once," thought Frank. So he returned home and threw out all of his lemonade.

Then he made some good lemonade. He sold every cup but one. That was the cup he gave to his little brother.

A Job for Ole Svenson

by Paul Tulien
illustrated by Len Epstein

Ole Svenson lived by himself. His wife had died, and his children had grown up and moved away. Ole was delighted that his children were independent, but he often missed them. Now that he'd retired from his job, he was especially lonely.

So Ole decided to get a new job. He inspected the ads in the paper. But once he saw that he was too old for most of the jobs, he laid the paper aside.

Then he remembered the employment agency. The agency had previously found him some work. Ole decided to see if they could help him again.

Ole went to the agency, but the man there shook his head. "I'm sorry," he said. "Most of the jobs we have are for younger men."

"Isn't there anything?"

"Let's see. A lady called and wanted someone to cut down a tree. But that's hard work."

"I've cut down many trees," Ole said. "I'm sure I could do it."

"All right," the man said. "I'll write down the address for you."

When Ole found the place, a woman opened the door.

"Good morning, Mrs. Allen," Ole said. "I'm Ole Svenson. The employment agency sent me."

"Come in, please," Mrs. Allen said. "I must leave right now. If you want to know about anything, Linda can tell you. She's the oldest. The two younger children are Carl and Nancy. Goodbye."

Ole and the children said goodbye, and the door closed behind her. Then Ole turned to Linda. "Will you show me which tree your mother wants cut down?"

Linda stared at him. "I didn't know she wanted a tree cut down."

"The man at the agency told me she did. Maybe I'd better wait until she comes back."

"Could you tell us a story while you wait?" Carl asked.

"Of course," Ole said. Hadn't he spent many hours telling stories to his own children?

Mrs. Allen came back a few hours later. The children were so involved in Ole's stories that they did not notice her right away.

"He tells very interesting stories," Linda said.

"The children didn't know which tree you wanted cut down," Ole said, "so I've been telling them stories."

Mrs. Allen looked puzzled. "I didn't want a tree cut down."

"The man at the agency said you did."

"Someone else must have wanted a tree cut down," Mrs. Allen said. "I asked for a babysitter. I suppose they got things mixed up."

Ole started for the door. "Well, I'll be going then."

"Wait a minute, Mr. Svenson. I haven't paid you yet."

"But I haven't done any work," Ole said.

"Of course you have! Babysitting is work."

"That's the easiest work I ever did," Ole declared. "I wish I could do it every day. The days get so lonely."

"I'm sure you could do it every day if people knew about you. Why don't you put an ad in the paper?"

So that's what Ole did, and his days are no longer lonely.

Wee Willie Goes Walking

by Carla Benedict
illustrated by Dave Blanchette

Michael wanted to earn some money. He wanted to buy a pair of ice skates. He had started a dog-walking business. So far that day he had walked a bulldog, a poodle, and a beagle. Now he was going to walk Ms. Silva's dog, Wee Willie.

Wee Willie was a Saint Bernard puppy who already weighed more than Michael. "Willie is very friendly, but he has lots of spirit. He gets excited easily," Ms. Silva warned. "If you can handle him, I'll let you walk him every day."

"I could use the extra money," said Michael. He fastened a leash to Willie's collar. He opened the screen door. Wee Willie scrambled for the sidewalk. He was dragging Michael behind him.

Suddenly a robin flew down from a treetop. It landed in their path. Before Michael could say, "No, Willie," the dog had jerked the leash out of Michael's hand. "Come back!" Michael cried, as Wee Willie went speeding after the bird.

Michael dashed down the alley after Willie, but soon he ran out of breath. He stopped near City Park. He wondered how he'd explain this to Ms. Silva. Just then he heard splashing and barking. It seemed to be coming from the park.

Michael ran through the park to the fountain. There he found Wee Willie jumping and biting at the water. Michael leaped into the fountain. The excited dog gave him a messy, wet kiss. Michael coaxed Wee Willie out of the fountain with a soggy dog biscuit.

"Ms. Silva," Michael began with a sigh when he finally got the dog home, "you may not believe this, but..."

"How thoughtful of you to give Willie a bath as well as a walk!" Ms. Silva said in a pleased voice. "You're hired to walk Wee Willie *every* day!"

Tracy's First Job

by Westley Donaldson
illustrated by Deborah White

Tracy told Joe about the bike she had seen for sale down the street. "It needs a new seat and some paint, but I think it's a bargain for twenty dollars," she said. "It will probably be sold before I can save that much money, though."

"I'm giving up my paper route," Joe said. "You could have that twenty dollars in no time if you took my route. Why don't we talk to Mr. Wise and see if it's OK?"

"Great!" Tracy said. "I can almost feel myself riding like the wind already."

Mr. Wise said it would be fine with him if Tracy took Joe's route. Then he asked Joe to show Tracy the route and explain the job.

That afternoon Joe showed Tracy how to fold and load the papers. He gave her hints about how to throw a paper so it landed right in front of the door. As they went through the route, Joe told her the name of each customer as he pointed out the houses on the route. "Maybe you should write down these names and addresses, Tracy," Joe said. "Some of these roads look alike."

"No, I don't need to. I have memory like a computer," Tracy said.

The next day Tracy did the paper route alone. She started at three o'clock. At 3:30 she was at the last house. "That was easy," she thought. "And I still have time to play before supper." But when she looked in her bag there was one more paper. Tracy had no idea where it belonged. How could she find out? Finally, she decided to call Joe to get addresses of all his customers. This time she wrote them down.

Tracy found that she had forgotten to give a paper to the Blair family. After the paper was delivered, she looked at her watch. It was time for supper.

"Well, I learned two things today," Tracy thought. "One, my memory is not as good as I thought. Two, I will save time if I do my route right the first time."

From Making Music to Making Food: Dreams That Change

by Joyce Mallery
illustrated by Barbara Kiwak

Ever since he can remember, John Haskell wanted to make music. "I had to tell him to leave the piano, put on a coat, and play outside," his mother remembers. John liked to practice the piano when he was young, usually an hour a day.

"When I was lonely, I would play the piano," he remembers. "My mother didn't have to nag me or argue. She didn't have to tell me the value of practice. I wanted to practice."

John began taking piano lessons when he was five years old. By the time he was in middle school, he played the piano in church and in the school band.

When John was in high school, he began to dream of making a living by playing the piano. He played the piano for music groups and joined rock-and-roll bands. "Few of my friends really understood my dream," recalls John. "My life was music."

No Longer a Dream

By the time John finished college, he was ready to make his dream a reality. He earned a living by playing the piano. He played in rock bands and played the organ at church. He gave piano lessons to children and played the piano for music groups. He also traveled to Japan, England, and Russia to play for opera groups. The piano was his voice.

"I loved it," he says. "I got to play wonderful music and meet lots of people. But it was also very hard work." He had to work nights and weekends and learn different kinds of music.

Changing Dreams

As John got older, his dream began to change. "I played the piano for over 30 years. It got harder to enjoy playing because I did it so much. I wanted to do different kinds of music, more as a hobby."

So, another dream began to grow. John always loved to cook and to try different kinds of food. His mother cooked for other people, and his grandfather owned a restaurant. He could remember the wonderful smells of food in his home and the glow on his mother's face when she cooked.

John decided to go back to school and become a chef. He learned how to bake and cook for large groups. He experimented with new kinds of food. He also had to learn how to cook safely and to keep a clean kitchen.

"I was 47 when I went back to school, and it was great!" he says. "I loved learning something new and spending days in the kitchen." He could also spend time writing his own music instead of playing the piano to earn a living.

Now John was ready to follow a new dream— to open his own restaurant. "I want to cook interesting food for people," he says. "I want to use fresh foods and to make food exciting."

"People change," he says. "Your view of life changes. I found out that you can follow many dreams during your life and make them come true!"

The Floating Market

by Winifred and Cecil Lubell

Most of us do our shopping in a supermarket. It's easy to shop there, and it's fast. But it's not much fun. You get a cart and push it along in front of you. Shelf after shelf goes by. They are piled with boxes and bottles and bags and tins. But there are no surprises. There is no excitement. It's just a bother.

Think how much fun it was to shop long, long ago. Then, people shopped in street markets. These were held in town squares. There were wagons and carts full of things to buy. Sellers called out loudly for buyers. "Buy my fruit!" "Here's a nice calf!" "Don't wait too long!" There were crowds of people. There may have been a cart selling sweets. Someone may have been selling balloons.

Markets like these have been known for thousands of years. They still take place today in many parts of the world.

One of the strangest markets is held in the city of Bangkok. That is the largest city of Thailand. It has a floating market. Instead of market stalls there are market boats.

Bangkok has many klongs, or waterways. They are used like streets. Houses and shops are built on tall poles along the banks of the klongs. In the middle of one of the klongs the floating market is held each morning. Sellers come out in sampans, small boats.

The sampans are loaded down with goods to be sold. Everything on the boats is placed in baskets. At one end of the boat sits the seller. This may be a woman wearing a wide straw hat that looks like a basket. There may be a shade in the boat to keep the sun and rain off the goods being sold.

The sellers move about looking for buyers. Some people shop from their boats. Others wait on the banks of the klong. There are hundreds of market sampans. Some carry fresh fruit, meat, animals, or flowers. Others hold dried fish, rice, cereal, or lentils in sacks. Some sell cloth or pots and pans, or pencils. There is an ice-cream boat. There is even a floating coffee shop.

The klong is very crowded. It's a wonder the sampans don't bump into each other. But that doesn't happen very often. The market sellers are careful as they move about and keep tabs on each other.

If you lived in Bangkok you might see this sort of market each day. You'd pass mail boats and police boats. You'd see sampans. You could watch the busy crowds. All round you there'd be noise and new sights to enjoy. And you might just be watching it all from the water-bus that was carrying you to school!

UNIT 2

Reading Reflections

These questions can help you think about the stories you just read. After you write your responses, discuss them with a partner.

Focus on the Characters

- Which character underestimated his or her talents while looking for a new job?
- Frank learned what sells lemonade after several days of failed attempts. Name another story in this unit where someone learned from his or her mistakes.
- Which characters in this unit were able to turn an unfortunate circumstance into an opportunity?

Focus on the Stories

- What talents did John Haskell use to create his dream jobs in "From Making Music to Making Food: Dreams that Change"?
- What are two ways that Frank tried to attract customers in "Good Lemonade"? Why do these ways fail to get more customers?
- Which selections show that hard work is an important part of turning a dream into a job?

Dreams to Jobs

Focus on the Theme

- People work at different jobs for different reasons. Name a selection in this unit where someone works to earn extra money. Name a selection in this unit where someone works to cure loneliness.
- Which selection in this unit is the best example of someone turning his or her dream into a job?
- Which job described in this unit would you most enjoy having?

The First Napkins

by Maria Leach
illustrated by Pat Morrison

There is an old riddle that asks, "Who sits at the king's table and doesn't use a napkin?" The answer is, "A fly." But long, long ago the king himself didn't use a napkin. He didn't even *have* one.

The king used to wipe his mouth on the tablecloth. In fact, everyone at the feast did the same thing. It was crude, but it worked.

The king's tablecloths were truly beautiful things. They were made from white damask. This was a cloth from the city of Damascus. The city was known for its fine weavers. Flowers and strange animals were woven into the cloth. Tablecloths were so rare and cost so much that each great household usually had only one, and it was used only when a special feast was held.

The people in those days took the food from the plates with their fingers. Then they would wipe their fingers on the tablecloth. They would wipe the goop off their chins. The wonderful white cloth would get dirtier and dirtier. After a few feasts it would be ruined. So the king would send men to Damascus to buy another, and they would come back with another gorgeous cloth.

But something had to be done. These fine cloths had to be saved from being spoiled. That is why English kings and lords began to use the *surnap*. The surnap was a little tablecloth placed at the king's end of the table. Two servants brought it in at the end of the feast. They knelt before the king and handed him the ends of it.

A servant brought the king a bowl of water known as a *laver*. The king dipped his hands into the water. Then he wiped them on the surnap. Only the king and queen used the surnap.

While the king was washing his hands and wiping them on the surnap, bowls of water and towels were carried to each of the guests. They dipped their hands into the water. They wiped them on the white linen towels. That was the beginning of napkins: a towel for each guest.

The Secret of Room 5

by Margaret Davidson

Once there was a boy named Thomas Edison. He was very curious and asked a lot of questions. The word he liked best was *why*. Sometimes he got answers to his questions. Sometimes he did not. But Tom did not stop asking. He wanted to know how each thing in the world worked.

Thomas Edison was born more than a hundred years ago. At that time there were no telephones. There were no cars. There were no radios. And there was not one electric light.

When Tom grew up, he worked out answers to his questions. Some of his answers were new inventions. One was "the talking machine," or phonograph. Another was the electric light. This story tells about one of Edison's other inventions—the secret of room 5.

Edison's electric light bulb.

Edison's "talking machine."

71

In 1887, Edison was hard at work.

In 1887 Edison was hard at work. He had come up with a really great idea, but he didn't want to tell anyone about it.

It was a secret because Tom had learned a painful lesson. Once he had talked about his plans to others. Those people had then used his ideas to make their own inventions. They claimed the ideas were theirs first.

He wouldn't be that careless again. So Edison kept this new plan a secret. He and his helpers worked very hard on it. They worked inside a locked room. No one else ever saw what they were doing. They called the plan "the secret of room 5."

Edison and his helpers did many tests. They made many models. Each model was better than the one before, but none of them was good enough. At last, after two years of careful work, Edison yelled, "We've got it! We've got it!"

The Edison Laboratory in West Orange, New Jersey.

Edison and his wife.

The secret was ready to be born. Edison had done his work well. Now he would let his helpers build the final model. He wanted a rest. So he and his wife left on a trip to Europe.

When they returned, his helpers met him. They took him to a room. They told him to sit down. A big machine was in the back of the room. Next to it was a phonograph.

Suddenly the room was plunged into darkness. A whirring sound filled the air. A light came from the strange machine. A picture appeared on the white wall in front of them. It was a picture of a man. He took off his hat and bowed. A voice came from the phonograph. It said, "Good day, Mr. Edison. Glad to see you back. I hope you are pleased."

The wonderful secret of room 5 was a film. Thomas Edison had made the first motion pictures.

Edison and the motion picture machine.

And Away We Go!

by Ann Poole
illustrated by Brock Nicol

On December 17, 1903, at Kitty Hawk, North Carolina, Wilbur and Orville Wright successfully flew their flying machine. Johnny Moore and his friends witnessed this great accomplishment.

Johnny Moore couldn't believe his luck. His father did not need him on the fishing boat that day. The sixteen-year-old could do whatever he wanted. And more than anything, Johnny wanted to watch the two men from Ohio work on their flying machine.

Orville and Wilbur Wright

Johnny ate a hasty breakfast. Then he raced over the sand dunes to Kill Devil Hill. He wasn't disappointed. The flag was waving over Orville and Wilbur Wright's camp. That meant that today, December 17, 1903, the Wright brothers would try to put the machine in the air. Four other men had already gathered on the narrow strip of sand. They were from the lifesaving station at Kitty Hawk. The Wrights had tried to fly their machine other times, but bad weather and last-minute mechanical problems had kept the machine on the ground.

"The weather doesn't look perfect," Johnny said to one of the men. He shivered in the frigid air.

"There's a bone-chilling wind. And it's cloudy," the man answered.

"Do you think they'll really fly it?" Johnny asked.

"I think they'll try. But I don't believe for a moment that it will go up," the man said.

"Most likely, it will turn over and put its nose in the sand," another man joined in.

"Better sand than trees," the fourth man said. "Kitty Hawk is the perfect place. Here there is protection from the wind, no trees, and plenty of firmly packed sand to soften a crash landing."

Now, everyone watched every movement as the Wrights put down tracks made of long wooden boards. They checked the wire wings. They made sure there were no holes in the cloth that covered the wire wings. They tested the engine one last time. They paid attention to every detail. The Wrights had built this engine themselves, as they had built every part of their flying machine. The engine was powerful, but it didn't weigh much.

Orville and Wilbur stood before the wooden machine. They tossed a coin. Johnny couldn't see whether it landed "heads or tails" side up. But Orville won the toss. He climbed onto the lower wing. He grabbed the controls. Wilbur let go of the tail. The machine began to move slowly along the track. Then it moved faster and faster. It reached the end of the track. The machine lifted up and into the air. It headed straight into a 21-mile-an-hour wind. The machine rose 10 feet above the ground. It traveled 100 feet before setting down gently on the sand. They had accomplished their mission.

Johnny ripped off his hat and threw it in the air.

"Well, what do you know!" one of the men said in amazement, astounded by what they had all just witnessed.

The flight had lasted only 12 seconds. But a man in a machine that weighed more than air had flown. Johnny and the other men watched as Wilbur took a turn. He flew 175 feet. Orville took another turn. Then Wilbur flew again. On that last flight, Wilbur flew 850 feet in 59 seconds.

At the end of the day, all five observers rushed up to the Wrights to shake their hands. These men were among the very few to see the new flying machine. The Wrights told the newspapers about their flight, but few printed the story. The papers that did report the event printed wrong information. Hardly anybody believed what they read about the Wrights' "flying." The idea was too hard to accept. Up until December 17, 1903, people just didn't fly.

Virginian-Pilot

VOL. XIX. NO. 68. NORFOLK, VA., FRIDAY, DECEMBER 18, 1903. TWELVE PAGES. THREE CENTS PER COPY.

12 Pages In Two Parts

FLYING MACHINE SOARS 3 MILES IN TEETH OF HIGH WIND OVER SAND HILLS AND WAVES AT KITTY HAWK ON CAROLINA COAST

TALLY SHEETS WILL DECIDE CONTEST

Chairman Dey Forced to Return From Richmond to Get Sheets For Committee

TREHY FACTION HAS ADVANTAGE THUS FAR

All Proxies Ruled Out of Meeting by Decisive Vote Before Fight Began

BOTH SIDES TO ABIDE BY FINAL DECISION

(Special to Virginian-Pilot.)
RICHMOND, VA., Dec. 17.—With all indications pointing to victory for the Trehy faction, the state executive committee, after spending the day hearing the Norfolk election contest, adjourned just before midnight until 10 o'clock tomorrow morning, after only recess, in which some radical action was taken. Meanwhile Chairman W. Dey, under instructions from the committee, left for Norfolk, accompanied by two deputies and by Police Commissioner Hurd. They are expected to return here in the morning and produce the tally sheets of the election of October 13, which Dey has declined to his safe in the seaside city. Aside from this, the important feature of the day was the passage of a resolution to lawful authority. With some spirit he repudiated any suggestion that he and his clients were of the class who ever refused to abide the decision of the duly constituted party authority.

Mr. Lawless, of counsel for petitioners, referred to the clause in the petition asking the chairman to request the...

U. S. LANDING PARTY FINDS STRONG CAMP OF COLOMBIAN TROOPS

Natives Order American Flag Hauled Down on Cutter But it Stays Put

(By Cable to Virginian-Pilot.)
COLON, Dec. 17.—The United States cruiser Atlanta, Commander William H. Turner, returned here last night from the Gulf of Darien. She discovered December 15 a detachment of Colombian troops numbering visually about 500 men, but according to their statements, totalling 1,500 to 2,000 men, at Titumati, on the western side of it just north of the mouth of the Atrato river. The commander of the Atlanta sent ashore an officer, who conversed with the Colombian commander. The latter protested energetically against the presence of an American warship in Colombian waters, in so much as it had become known that Panama had not been declared, and politely requested the Atlanta to leave the Gulf, because it belonged to Colombia. Commander Turner removed the request, and the Atlanta returned to Colon to report to Rear Admiral Coghlan. The Colombians are clearly busy with preventive and actively busy with precautions. Although they treated the Americans courteously they decidedly resented the presence of the Atlanta's landing party. The Colombian force was composed of the men landed recently at the Atrato river by the Colombian cruisers Cartagena and General Pinzon.

Early in the morning of December 15 the Atlanta sighted a small schooner in the center of the Gulf of Darien and followed her to the western shore, where the schooner attempted to hide behind an islet. Lieutenant Havier P. Perrill, of the Atlanta, was ordered to board her and thereupon a whaleboat was lowered and pulled towards the schooner.

It was found that the schooner had on board a hundred Colombian soldiers, commanded by General Rafael Novo, who and General Daniel Ortiz, commander-in-chief of the Colombian forces of the Atlantic and the Pacific, had a large camp a mile away, on the mainland. General Novo requested Lieutenant Perrill to land and confer with General Ortiz. After temporarily returning to the Atlanta, Lieutenant Perrill went back to the schooner, which in the meantime had taken a position off a beach within a small bay. Great excitement prevailed among the Colombians on the whaleboat's approach. There were repeated cries of "Viva Colombia," and there was a sudden concentration of about 120 Colombian soldiers on the beach. For some moments the situation appeared dangerous and had the appearance of ambuscade. General Ortiz appeared on the beach when Lieutenant Perrill went ashore, the whaleboat in the meantime lying close to the beach. General Ortiz insisted that Lieutenant Perrill should fly the Colombian flag at the bow of the whaleboat, or lower the American flag at her stern, because she was in Colombian waters.

Lieutenant Perrill replied that he did not leave a Colombian flag on board to lower the stars and stripes. General Ortiz did not insist upon his so doing, but he protested in writing against the presence of the Americans in Colombian waters. Lieutenant Perrill accepted the protest and conveyed it to Commander Turner, who handed it to Rear Admiral Coghlan on his arrival here. General Ortiz and others freely expressed the determination of Colombia to fight to the bitter end in case General Reyes' visit to Washington is not successful and Panama is not returned to Colombia.

COTTON TRADE TO DEFEAT COTTON

TO DEEPEN THE HARBOR AT NORFOLK

Secretary of War to Report Plan to Congress For Making Ship Channel Here 35 Feet Deep to Float Big Warships

SENATOR MARTIN INTRODUCED MEASURE

(Special to Virginian-Pilot.)
Washington, Dec. 17.—Senator Martin introduced and had passed today a resolution directing the secretary of war to have made a survey of Norfolk harbor with an estimate of the cost, by which there may be obtained a channel of 35 feet from deep water to the navy yard, and also the cost of a channel 35 feet deep. The channel is in places only 23 feet deep, and the department considers that there is always some fear that a warship will strike one of these shallows when coming into the navy yard.

All of the Atlantic ports are now clamoring to have the depth of waters in their harbors increased, so as to accommodate the increased size of modern ships. The best item in Norfolk and of the Norfolk navy yard in this respect are as important as those of any other Atlantic port. Looking at the matter from a naval standpoint, the increase of the Norfolk navy yard has for some time been taking a deep interest in the matter. Last spring Senator Martin, invited by the commercial bodies of the city of Norfolk to make a personal inspection of the harbor and the channel, it from deep water, with a view to considering what could be done to secure...

"WANTS CANAL BUILT WITHOUT SUSPICION OF NATIONAL DISHONOR"

Senator Hoar and Gorman in Fiery Debate on Floor of the Senate

(By Telegraph to Virginian-Pilot.)
WASHINGTON, DEC. 17.—The senate today was the scene of a most important debate on the isthmian canal question as affected by the president's recognition of the independence of the republic of Panama. The discussion began with a speech by Mr. Hoar on his resolution of inquiry and lasted several hours. In addition to Mr. Hoar's address there were speeches by Mr. Gorman and Mr. Foraker. All three were notable utterances and of historical interest.

Mr. Hoar confined his remarks to his resolution, and they were carefully written out and read from manuscript. He held that this country has not yet received full official information concerning the isthmian revolution, and criticized in sharp terms the conduct of this country as shown by what has been given out.

There was no reservation in Mr. Gorman's utterances. He practically alleged that the situation in Panama had been created to make a campaign issue, and said that unless further information was thrown on the subject, he would oppose the Panama treaty.

Mr. Foraker took Mr. Hoar to task severely for his remarks reflecting on the administration. He defended the administration. Its attitude toward the Panama revolt. A heated colloquy took place between Mr. Foraker and Mr. Hoar during an effort of the Massachusetts senator to explain more fully his position in the matter.

Mr. Hoar said he was in favor of the isthmian canal, but was anxious that the canal should be built "without taint or suspicion of national dishonor."

"What we want to know is," he said, "did this government, knowing that a revolution was about to take place, so arrange matters that the revolution, whether peaceable or otherwise, should be permitted to go on without molestation, and whether our national authorities took measures to prevent Colombia from stopping it."

Mr. Hoar quoted the correspondence bearing upon the revolution, and asked, "Why this great anxiety before any disturbance had occurred?" If, he said,... a man about to attack another, is justified, before the blow is struck, in manacling the assailed party, and made the policeman to have been taking the pocketbook which has been taken from the victim by the assailant should be turned over to him the policeman on the ground that he was the rightful owner?"

Mr. Gorman took the floor as soon as Mr. Hoar had concluded, and there was from the start evident interest in what he might say. He began with reference to Mr. Hoar's speech and complimented that senator highly on his attitude and alluded to the democratic attitude on the canal question. On the point said that all democratic senators generally are as favourable to the construction of the canal as are republicans. Mr. Gorman said the facts were all that were desired, and he proceeded to refer to the suspension of the sabre habeas corpus, saying that that influence had been extended from time to time until "the senate had become practically the agent of the executive."

The affair in Panama, he declared, "was the most flagrant act of transgression that has ever taken place in the history of our country, and it should be restored without regard to party."

Mr. Gorman criticized Mr. Loomis for his discussion of the Panama situation at a New York banquet before injunction of secrecy had been removed by the senate. Mr. Gorman said Mr. Loomis had discussed the Panama situation, a banquet at which perhaps many were excited by wine, and had given information which the senate had given him under the administration or from any source. He did not, Mr. Gorman continued, "call this country all the facts, but he made the broad assertion that the president was a bold and great man, who had had his own course and the patriotism to land marines and seize a part of the territory of the republic of Colombia, which we were under contract to guarantee to that country. This," he added, "in the light of the facts before us, nothing less than usurpation."

Mr. Gorman then discussed the president as a "second Napoleon," which...

NO BALLOON ATTACHED TO AID IT

Three Years of Hard, Secret Work by Two Ohio Brothers Crowned With Success

ACCOMPLISHED WHAT LANGLEY FAILED AT

With Man as Passenger Huge Machine Flew Like Bird Under Perfect Control

BOX KITE PRINCIPLE WITH TWO PROPELLERS

The problem of aerial navigation without the use of a balloon has been solved at last.

Over the sand hills of the North Carolina coast yesterday, near Kitty Hawk, two Ohio men proved that they could soar through the air in a flying machine of their own construction, with the power to steer it and speed it at will. This, too, in the face of a wind blowing at the registered velocity of twenty-one miles an hour.

Like a monster bird the invention hovered above the breakers and circled over the rolling sand hills at the command of its navigator and, after soaring for three miles, it gracefully de...

Where Do We Get All That Paper?

by Elsie Sea

illustrated by Alexander Farquharson

What do a birthday card, a milk carton, and a movie ticket have in common? They are all made of paper. Paper is everywhere. We use it every day. But that was not always the case.

Long ago, people did not have paper. They wrote on soft clay and let it dry. They carved words into stone. They painted on walls. They wrote on animal skins. There was no easy way to keep records because there were no books.

The word *paper* comes from Egypt. At one time, the Egyptians took a plant called papyrus and cut it into thin strips. They put these strips side by side. Then they pounded the strips together. This made a kind of paper. But making papyrus paper was awfully hard work. People made one sheet at a time and there were many flaws.

The kind of paper we use today was invented in China. In A.D. 105, a man named Ts'ai Lun worked for the emperor. He was a recorder of records. People in China wrote on silk and bamboo.

Ts'ai Lun sought something better to write on. He took pieces of old rope, rags, tree bark, and rotting fishnet. He soaked them in water. He pounded the mixture with a club to make a soft pulp. He poured the pulp into a mold, which squeezed out the water. When the pulp was dry, he opened the mold. He had made the world's first sheet of paper.

For five hundred years, the Chinese were the only people who knew how to make paper. Then other people learned about papermaking. They were taught by Chinese merchants and migrant craftsmen.

For many years, all paper was made from rags. It was still made one sheet at a time. Then, in 1798, a Frenchman invented a machine that made paper in rolls. Papermaking was now much faster. Not only was pounding rags into pulp too slow, but finding enough rags was too expensive. Soon, in Europe and America, people learned to make paper from wood pulp.

Now, almost all paper is made from wood. Trees are cut and the bark is removed. The wood is mixed with water and made into pulp. Then the pulp goes through the papermaking machine. First, the pulp is poured onto a mesh belt. Most of the water drains out. Then the paper moves to rollers. The rollers squeeze out more water and press the paper flat. Some machines can make 3,000 feet (900 meters) of paper a minute. It took many specialists including chemists and machinists to perfect the process.

Think of all the things you use that are made of paper. Writing paper, wrapping paper, books, paper plates, boxes, paper bags, newspapers, tissues, and paper towels are some of them. We can thank the Chinese for paper, one of the most popular inventions of all time.

The First Foghorn

by Lucy Bowdler
illustrated by Alexander Farquharson

One night many years ago, a music teacher named Robe Foulis had to find his way home by ear. A thick fog had covered the town. Foulis could hardly see the lights in the windows of the houses. But he was sure he could find his house. This was the time of evening when his daughter practiced on the piano. Even if he couldn't see his house, he would hear her playing scales or a song.

As he got near home, he heard the sound of the piano, all right. But something was wrong. His daughter seemed to be playing just one note, over and over again.

Robe Foulis stood outside his gate. He was puzzled. What was wrong with his daughter's music tonight?

Then he walked through the gate and up the steps. Now he could hear the other notes in the scale.

He went into the house and into the living room. "Play the scale again," he said. "Keep playing it, very slowly, until I come in again."

He went back into the fog. He walked about a hundred feet from the house. The only notes he heard now were those in the lower half of the scale.

He walked farther away. Again he stopped to listen. Again the only notes he heard were those in the lower half of the scale.

He walked on. A thousand feet from the house he stopped. He could hear only one note—the lowest one of all!

Foulis ran all the way home. He knew he had made an important discovery. Fog not only makes things hard to see. It blots out many noises as well. But some sounds can cut through the fog.

That night he began to build a small steam whistle. It would sound the same low note he had heard from the piano. Some people laughed when they learned what he was making. They considered it a toy. But that didn't stop him.

At last Foulis finished the whistle. He set it up at a place called Partridge Island. This was at the entrance to St. John Harbor, on the east coast of Canada, where Foulis lived. A man stayed with the whistle and kept a steam boiler going so that the whistle would blow.

A week later another fog came to St. John. No ships could move without being in danger. Hardly a sound could be heard. But then, through the thick fog, came the sound of Foulis's whistle to guide the ships.

Sailors did not laugh at the music teacher's invention. They knew their ships would be safer now. Today foghorns can be heard in all waters where ships must travel through fog. Lighthouses, buoys, and ships employ the foghorn. It warns other ships and boats not to come too close.

What's in a Name?

by Alex Petrovic
illustrated by Gary Torrisi

The earl of Sandwich was an English nobleman who liked to play games. One day, he was having a fine time playing at a game table. "This is fun," he exclaimed. "I don't want to stop." But he hadn't eaten for a while and was getting hungry. He needed some food but didn't want to stop playing to get a meal. Well, you know how it is. When you're having fun, you don't want to stop. Right?

So the earl instructed a servant to bring him what he needed. "Bring me some meat," he said. "Or some cheese. Put it between two pieces of bread. I'll eat it right here, and I'll go on playing." And so he did. This way of eating worked so well that he kept it up. He did it often, and it became a habit. His friends talked about it. They found a name for two pieces of bread with some other food between them.

What was the name? *Sandwich*, of course. They gave it the name of the man who liked to eat that way. That's how the sandwich got its name.

Now, another English nobleman was the earl of Cardigan. He had some sweaters, but he didn't like to pull them over his head. Perhaps they mussed his hair. Perhaps they strained his back. It doesn't matter.

Anyway, he didn't like to pull them on. So he went to his tailor. "Make me some sweaters with buttons down the front," he instructed the tailor. "I'll put them on like shirts, and I'll button them up."

So the tailor constructed just such a sweater. And what did he call them? Why, *cardigans*, of course. He named the button-up sweater after the earl who thought of it. And that's how the cardigan sweater got its name.

But think of this. What if the earl of Cardigan had been too busy for meals? What if *he* had eaten quick snacks between bread? And what if the earl of Sandwich had disliked pullover sweaters? What if *he* had asked for one with buttons?

You know the answer. It's easy. We'd eat cardigans, we'd wear sandwiches, and we wouldn't mind at all! Only the names would be different.

101

UNIT 3

Reading Reflections

These questions can help you think about the stories you just read. After you write your responses, discuss them with a partner.

Focus on the Characters

- How did it feel for Johnny Moore to watch the first flight of the Wright Brothers?
- Why was it necessary for Thomas Edison to be so secretive about his inventions?
- Do you think Robe Foulis would have invented the foghorn if he had not been a music teacher? Why or why not?

Focus on the Stories

- How were the Wright brothers and Thomas Edison alike?
- As explained in "The First Napkins," the invention of the napkin evolved over time. Name another selection in this unit that discusses how an invention was improved upon over time.
- The napkin resulted from a king's request. Name another story that shows the influences of royalty on inventions.

What an Idea!

Focus on the Theme

- Inventions come from different sources. Sometimes they are created in order to fulfill a need. In which selections were inventions created in order to fulfill a need? In which selections were inventions mainly the result of the inventor's curiosity?
- People had a hard time accepting the idea that the Wright brothers could fly. Name another story in this unit where the inventor was laughed at or not believed.
- Which do you think is the best idea discussed in this unit? Explain your choice.

Nine-Day Nightmare

by Jacques Verdol
illustrated by Yvonne Gilbert

A few years ago a plane crashed in the thick jungles of Brazil in South America. Some people were killed. Others were later rescued near the plane. But one person was missing. She was Juliana Koepks, seventeen years old. She was not found among the living or the dead. But Juliana was alive. In the following paragraphs she tells what happened.

The plane was flying smoothly when all at once I felt a crashing blow. I was in the air going head over heels but still strapped in my seat. Then I passed out.

I came to in the rain. It was still daylight. I was alone, surrounded by huge trees. I had lost a shoe during the fall, and my foot was causing me a great deal of pain.

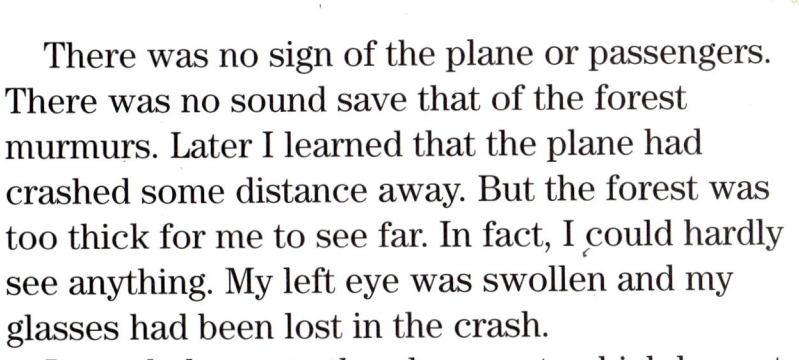

There was no sign of the plane or passengers. There was no sound save that of the forest murmurs. Later I learned that the plane had crashed some distance away. But the forest was too thick for me to see far. In fact, I could hardly see anything. My left eye was swollen and my glasses had been lost in the crash.

I crawled over to the plane seat, which lay not far away, and spent the night there. The seat was softer than the ground, but I did not sleep much.

The next morning I decided that I just couldn't stay there waiting for help that might never come. So I started walking. But first I picked up a long stick to tap the ground before me to chase away poisonous spiders and snakes. Those things frightened me more than the idea of meeting wild beasts. The worst part was not being able to see well. I moved like a blind person, holding my arms out in front of me. Every ten or fifteen steps I had to stop and rest.

That day I crossed a little stream and decided to follow it. I thought it would flow into a river and lead me to people sooner or later.

When night came, I stretched out under a tree. I didn't sleep any better than I had the night before. But deep in my pocket I found some sweets. I ate a piece when I couldn't stand the hunger. I ate the last one on the fourth day.

The mosquitoes bothered me all the time. My arms, legs, and face were swollen and itchy. I became so tired I could hardly put one foot before the other. But before long I came to the junction of my little stream and a larger river. That gave me hope and courage.

To ease the thirst and hunger, I often drank from the river. But I had to drink quickly. First I beat the water with my stick to scare away the piranha. These are tiny fish, but they have sharp teeth and eat flesh.

As the days passed, I walked more and more slowly. My legs felt like iron weights. The heat was terrible. I was so hurt and exhausted that at times I didn't really know whether I was awake or in some nightmare.

On the ninth day I was just about to lie down and give up when my heart gave a leap. There on the riverbank was a canoe. Then I saw a cabin. I ran. Well, I tried to run, but in fact I stumbled along.

I went into the cabin and saw a bed, but I didn't have the strength to reach it. I fell to the floor in a faint.

A short time later two fishermen found me, and before long a helicopter took me to the Brazilian capital. My parents soon joined me, and the doctors told me that I would soon be completely recovered.

Strong in the Saddle

by Ann Murray
illustrated by Linda Pierce

It was January of 1994. Debbie Gadus and her friend Emily were in a barn at a riding stable. Suddenly, the roof collapsed. The girls couldn't get out of the way in time. The roof fell on them.

The girls lay under the roof. Both were in great pain. Emily told Debbie a fairy tale. This kept Debbie calm. Rescue workers finally dug them out. They took the girls to the hospital.

Emily had many broken bones, but she healed quickly. She was better after a few months.

Debbie wasn't as lucky. She had hurt her back. The talented horseback rider could not move or feel her legs. She spends much of her life in a wheelchair.

But Debbie wouldn't let her injuries stop her. She made a promise to her friend Emily. Debbie promised that one day, she would ride horses with Emily again. Debbie did not want to disappoint Emily.

About a year after the accident, Debbie asked her doctors to let her ride. She begged and begged until they decided to allow it. "Even then I had to twist their arms," she said.

Now Debbie goes to a special riding stable. It is for people who have had accidents like hers. At the stable, she rides a horse named Star. She rides him once a week for an hour.

Riding is hard when you can't feel your legs. Debbie still needs help to ride. She is learning to stay on Star's back. She does exercises to help her balance. Slowly, Debbie is getting stronger.

Debbie's coach has helped her ride. "We're just amazed," she says. "We're very proud of Debbie."

Debbie enjoys learning to ride again. The smile on her face as she sits in Star's saddle shows that. Debbie knows that someday she will keep her promise to Emily. It's only a matter of time before she will join Emily on a ride.

Debbie works in the office at the stable when she's not riding. One day, Debbie hopes to teach at the stable. Then she can help others to ride again.

Water Crushes Steel

by Nick Ramirez
illustrated by Pat Paris

My father takes a golf cart to the bow. It's too far to walk. He's the captain of one of the largest oil tankers in the world. She's called the *Petrol Princess.* She's longer than four football fields. It takes five miles just to stop her once she gets going.

On my thirteenth birthday, my birthday present was a ride on the *Petrol Princess.* My mom didn't want me to go. But my dad promised a short run from Baltimore to Quebec. The sea was calm when we left. It was actually very boring.

Unexpected Problems

Then the rudder broke. That's the part that steers the ship. It wouldn't move. We had to turn the engines off. We drifted free while Dad and his men tried to fix the rudder. It's the size of a huge billboard, and they couldn't move it.

They told the Coast Guard to keep other ships out of the way. We were far out at sea. There was little chance of hitting any land, so we didn't worry. Sooner or later, the men would fix the rudder, and we'd be fine. As long as the weather held, we could drift almost forever.

Rough Seas

Then a small, rainy storm off to the south hit a cold front. The two became a hurricane. The waves rose from ten feet to fifty in a few hours. The wind blew for all it was worth. The rain hit the windows like bullets. The steel wires that held up the radio antenna started humming. Their sound told my dad the wind was nearly a hundred miles an hour.

The huge ship rode up the front of each wave like a toy boat. As the wave broke, tons of water smashed down on the deck. Then the *Petrol Princess* would race down the back of the monster wave. We'd plow into the water. The whole ship would shake.

Without a rudder to keep us steady, the wind threw the giant ship around like a stick in a river. Then a rogue wave smashed into us. A rogue wave is one in a thousand. It broke the windows in the control room one hundred and ten feet up. The weight of all that water ripped the steel doors off. The ocean poured into the inside of my father's beautiful ship.

Help Arrives

She was sinking fast. We put on our life preservers. Then we climbed into lifeboats. The Coast Guard helicopters arrived. The wind blew them around like insects. One by one, they lifted us off the lifeboats by a cable. It was the scariest thing I ever did. My dad was last. It broke my dad's heart to see the *Petrol Princess* disappear under the final big wave.

On our way back to land, my dad turned to me. He said that for my fourteenth birthday, we'd go miniature golfing.

The Rooster and the Fox

Aesop's fable retold by Alan Samuels
illustrated by Judith Moffatt

One day when the world was young and the animals still talked like people, a rooster flew to the top of a tree. The morning sun shone like braided gold. The air was warm. The rooster felt so good, he began to sing. His song wasn't beautiful, but it was loud.

It was so truly loud, in fact, that it woke a fox some distance away. The fox woke up hungry. He wanted some breakfast. He thought that the rooster would make him a fine meal. So he set out to find him.

The fox came to the tree. He saw the rooster at the very top. Now foxes are clever, but they can't climb trees. He saw that he would have to trick the rooster into coming down.

He smiled up at the rooster. "How nice to see you!" he called genially. "I'm longing for some company. Why don't you come down? We could have a nice, friendly talk."

Now the rooster was not a fool. He knew exactly what the fox wanted, but he didn't say so. Instead, he said, "Why thank you! I'd love to. But I'd better not. I'm safe up here, you see.

"Oh, I know *you* wouldn't harm me. *You* just want to talk. But what if the hungry wolf came along? Or the cruel lion? They would be big trouble!"

"No, no, my friend," said the fox. "Haven't you heard the exciting news? There was a big meeting of the animals. It was decided that all animals will be friends from now on. No more eating each other! Peace has been made forever!"

"That's wonderful!" said the rooster. And then his eyes grew as wide as saucers as he looked off into the distance. He seemed very excited by what he saw, and he craned his neck as if to get a better look.

"What is it?" asked the fox. "What do you see?"

"More friends are coming!" said the rooster. "What fun! It's a big pack of dogs, running very fast. They'll be here any minute! Perhaps we can all have a party!"

The fox's smile vanished. He took off like an arrow.

The rooster called after him, "Where are you going? You aren't afraid of the dogs, are you? Have you forgotten that all the animals are friends now?"

But by now the fox was just a dot on the horizon.

And the dogs? Well, they never showed up. And that's how the rooster outfoxed the fox and lived to tell about it.

Emperors of the Ice

by Rona Lee Kleiman

When summer warms the Northern Hemisphere, it is winter down in Antarctica. And there, in the coldest place on Earth, emperor penguins lay and hatch their eggs.

Antarctica lies near the South Pole. Masses of snow and ice cover the land. Almost no plants or animals live there in the ultracold. The penguins that nest there must find food in the sea. But the hard life suits the emperors.

Other kinds of penguins build nests of sticks or rocks. But in the Antarctic there is only ice. Emperor penguins don't make nests. Instead, each bird has a special flap for holding eggs. The flap is found on the lower part of the bird's belly.

The coldest place on Earth.

Emperor penguins don't make nests.

In early winter the mother penguin lays a single egg. Soon after she lays the egg, she turns it over to her mate. She helps move the egg onto his feet. He will hold it there under his flap and keep it warm. When the chick hatches, he will feed it a milky food that is made in his throat.

Meanwhile the mother bird sets out for the sea. She has not eaten for a long time. She is hungry.

The trip to the sea is a very long one. It would take much longer if the penguins had to walk the whole way. But they have found a quicker way to travel. Throwing themselves down on their bellies, penguins can scoot across the ice. They dig their claws into the ice and push. Then they use their little wings for balance.

At the edge of the ice the females dive into the sea. There they feed on fish and microscopic sea creatures. After the females have eaten their fill, they do not stop eating. They fill sacs in their throats with food for the new chicks that they've never seen.

The trip to the sea is a long one.

Penguins have found a quicker way to travel.

After two months the mothers return to the chicks. Now it's father's turn. He and the other males have waited patiently for the females to return. They have not eaten anything but some nibbles of snow. Now they make the same long trip to the sea. Soon the mothers run out of food. But the fathers will return with more food for the hungry young. The parents take turns going back and forth to the sea.

125

Blizzards are a great danger to the chicks. When the first warning winds swirl about their feet, the penguins all crowd together. As many as six thousand penguins may stand in a circle. In the middle are the chicks. During a storm the snow may completely cover the chicks. But the circle helps keep them warm. Alone, a chick would freeze in a storm. A baby penguin is no match for the icy winds of an Antarctic blizzard.

By October, summer is on its way. The ice begins to thaw and break up. Soon the young penguins travel to the sea. And they, too, must hunt for food in the icy sea.

During a blizzard, the penguins all crowd together.

Emperor penguins hunt for food in the icy sea.

Dolphin Rescue

Based on a true story and
retold by Rebecca Brandenberg
illustrated by Joe Boddy

    It was a cool, winter morning off the coast of Florida. A diver wore a wet suit, an air tank, and flippers. He rolled over the side of his boat, splashed into the water, and drifted deep below the sea. He sensed that something might be about to happen.

    Suddenly, the diver heard a loud, clicking sound followed by a whistle. The clicking grew louder and louder until it pounded in his ears. It sounded just like a creaking door. Then, he saw three dolphins swimming quickly toward him—a father, a mother, and a baby. The baby dolphin's tail had become entangled in a huge ball of fishing line.

The little dolphin appeared scared and hurt, but its parents brought it even closer to the diver. They stopped about three feet away from him. What did those clicking noises mean? What were they trying to tell him? Were they asking for help?

The dolphins inched even closer. They allowed the diver to touch them. The parents held the baby between their flippers. They placed it on the sand in front of him. Suddenly, the frightened baby tried to swim away, but its parents brought it back. Using his beak, or nose, the father nudged the diver's arm upward a few times. It was as if he were urging him to "start working."

Despite their appearance, dolphins are not fish, but mammals, like people. If they become sick or injured in water, they may drown. The diver knew that without his help the baby dolphin could not swim and would probably die.

But could he really free the baby from the huge ball of tangled line? He took off his gloves and stroked the baby's smooth, silky skin. Suddenly, the three dolphins swam away. The parents swam under the injured baby, helping to support it. They returned a minute later. The diver realized that they had gone to the surface to breathe. "I'll have to work fast," he thought.

The fishing line cut into the baby dolphin's skin. The dolphin cried as the diver tried to gently loosen the line. The father clicked. He seemed to want the diver to work faster.

He worked carefully with his diving knife to try to liberate the baby. The mother dolphin stroked her baby with her nose. She hovered near it like a nurse. The father nudged the diver impatiently. Finally, the baby dolphin's tail was free. The parents clicked excitedly, and they swam rapidly toward the surface.

Floating above was a fishing boat. The father dolphin slapped his tail hard on top of the water. The surprised pair of fishers heard the warning. They headed toward shore. The dolphin chirped and whistled to his family. Then, they dove back below the waves.

When they returned, the three dolphins circled the diver. They clicked. The father looked into his eyes. He nudged the diver with his nose, as if to say "thank you." Then he clicked again, and the family again swam toward the surface.

In the days that followed, the diver couldn't stop thinking about the dolphins. Had the baby survived? Then one day, he spotted some dolphins racing near his boat. He heard a familiar whistle. Through his telescope he saw the baby dolphin swimming in the middle of the group! He watched with joy as the little dolphin leaped happily through the waves.

UNIT 4

Reading Reflections

These questions can help you think about the stories you just read. After you write your responses, discuss them with a partner.

Focus on the Characters

- Why did Emily tell Debbie a fairy tale while they were trapped under the barn roof in "Strong in the Saddle"?
- In "The Rooster and the Fox," the animals were able to talk. Name another selection in this unit where animals seemed to communicate.
- List three items that you think Juliana Koepks may have wished for during her "Nine-Day Nightmare." Explain your choices.

Focus on the Stories

- Why was it surprising that the *Petrol Princess* sank in "Water Crushes Steel"?
- How are the penguins in "Emperors of the Ice" similar to the dolphins in "Dolphin Rescue"?
- What actions did Juliana Koepks take in "Nine-Day Nightmare" that helped her survive?

Surviving

Focus on the Theme

- People must often overcome nature. Name a story in this unit where people must survive in spite of nature.
- Often people (and animals) are able to survive by helping one another. Name a story where this is true. However, sometimes there is no help, and people or animals have to survive on their own. Name a story in this unit where a character relies on himself or herself to survive.
- What did these selections tell you about what it takes to survive in a difficult situation?

How Lisa Learns to Talk

by Edna S. Levine
illustrated by Yemi

Most children learn words by hearing them. A small girl hears her father say, "Say daddy." The child hears the word over and over, listens carefully, makes the sounds in the word, and finally tries to say *daddy* herself. She hears her father say the word and learns to put the word together. And that is the way most children learn the words they say. They hear the words, practice making the different sounds, and then make words from those sounds.

But some children cannot learn to talk this way. They are children who cannot hear. One such child is Lisa. She will never be able to hear as well as other people. Lisa can hear just a little with a hearing aid. The hearing aid is quite small and weighs little.

There are special teachers, though, who help children who cannot hear to learn about words and talking. Lisa has such a teacher.

Lisa is learning to lipread. It is easy to misread what people are saying. She watches the lips and face of the person who is talking. She tries to understand what the person is saying from the way the person's lips move. Lisa is learning to see what people say.

Lipreading is very hard. Many words look the same on the lips. It is hard to tell them apart. Many people do not talk carefully. It is hard to see what they are saying, and there are many words that Lisa cannot lipread because she does not know what they mean. Lisa enjoys learning to lipread. When she grows up, she will be able to lipread many of the words that you are able to hear.

Lisa must also learn to talk. This is very hard to do when you can't hear how words sound. But Lisa learned that you can feel words. This may sound illogical, but it isn't.

When you say a word out loud, it makes a vibration in your nose or throat. Try it yourself. Put your hands on your throat and say *go*. Feel the vibration it makes. Say *summer* and feel the vibration on the side of your nose. Different words make different vibrations in different places.

When Lisa is learning to say a word, she puts her hands on her teacher's throat or nose. When her teacher says a word, Lisa feels the vibrations it makes. Then she tries to get the same vibrations herself when she says the word.

Lisa also has to watch her teacher's face, mouth, and lips. She sees how the word looks when her teacher says it and also listens with her hearing aid to hear as much as she can.

Lisa puts all these things together and tries to say the word herself. She says it over and over again until the teacher tells her she is saying it right. Because Lisa can't hear herself very well, autocorrection is not possible. The teacher must tell her when she is saying it right. A computer can also tell her when she says a word right. First the computer shows a picture of the sound the teacher makes when she says a certain word. Then the computer shows the sound Lisa makes when she says the same word. Lisa tries to say the word so that her sound-picture looks like the teacher's sound-picture.

This is a very hard way to learn to talk. Not all deaf children can do it. Even when Lisa talks, her voice does not sound the same as that of a hearing person. Sometimes it is hard to understand what Lisa says. With practice, however, Lisa's speech will continue to get better, making it easier for everyone to understand her.

Can Windmills Talk?

by Allan Walldren
illustrated by Barbara Kiwak

Do you know what a windmill is? Look at the pictures closely. They show windmills with their arms in four different positions. Most windmills have four arms. When the wind blows, it turns those giant arms. This turns a big stone inside the mill. The stone grinds grain. It turns the grain into flour. Farmers bring their grain to the mill. The miller makes it into flour. Then people bake bread with the flour. There are many windmills like these in Holland. Windmills are a great benefit to people.

Do you think windmills can talk? Well, they can. No, they don't speak words. Of course not. But they can talk with their arms. Here's how it works.

When the arms are not turning, the miller can leave them in any position. He can leave them in position 1. Or in position 2. Or in position 3. Or in position 4. Each position means something different. It's like hanging out a sign. It's a way of telling people about the mill.

Suppose the arms are in position 1. That shows that the mill is working. It has only stopped for a little while. Maybe the miller is having lunch. He'll be right back. So the farmers bring their grain to the mill. The miller promotes business this way.

But suppose the arms are in position 2. That shows that the mill is not working. It will be closed for a long time. Maybe the miller has some sort of malady or illness. Maybe he has gone on a trip. Maybe something is wrong with the mill. So farmers do not bring grain to that mill.

Perhaps you've seen a flag flying at half-mast. (That means halfway up the pole.) Flags are flown at half-mast to show sadness when an important person dies. In Holland people do the same kind of thing, but with windmills. They put the windmill arms in position 4 to show sadness. But for happy events, the arms are set in position 3.

In World War II, German soldiers invaded Holland. The Germans did not want any messages to be sent out of the country. They took over the radio stations. They listened in on people's phone calls. But the people of Holland still sent messages. How? They used their windmills, and they used a code. Each position of the arms had a special meaning.

By putting the windmill arms in certain positions, they sent messages to England. English pilots would fly over Holland. They would look at certain windmills. They knew the code. They could decipher the windmills' messages. They took the news back to England. The Germans didn't know about this code. They didn't know what was going on.

Can windmills talk? Indeed they can. If you know their language, they can tell you a lot.

The Horse Who Could Count

by Helen Kay
illustrated by Janice Skivington

There was once an amazing horse named Hans. He could read. He could count. He could even add.

Hans could not speak, of course. He answered questions by moving his head for *yes* and for *no*. He tapped the ground to spell. For *A* he tapped once. Two taps meant *B*, and so on.

His owner, Mr. Easter, believed that horses could learn just like people. One just had to teach them.

He would hold Hans's leg and tap it on the ground once for *A*. When he said *B*, he would tap the horse's leg twice, and so on through the alphabet. This went on for nearly two years. At last he did not have to move the horse's leg. He would call out a letter. The horse would tap it out. Each time Hans would get a lump of sugar.

People came from far and wide to see the famous horse. "How much is six and six?" they would ask the horse. They held their breath as Hans began to tap. At twelve taps, they broke into cheers. "What a clever horse!" they cried.

A group of professors from a large university was not so sure. They came to visit. They asked Hans questions. Each time the horse tapped out the right answer.

One such professor watched Hans. He considered what he saw improbable. Was it possible, he wondered, that the horse was getting a sign from people? Perhaps they gave signs without knowing it.

The man stepped behind a screen. Then he asked Hans a question. The horse could hear him, but he couldn't see him.

Hans began to tap. He tapped and tapped. He didn't know when to stop! He failed. He was asked another question. Again he failed. He couldn't give the right answer to any question.

The secret was out. Hans *was* a clever horse. But he didn't really know all the answers. He just tapped until he saw some sign that told him to stop.

Mr. Easter didn't know he was giving a sign. Nor did the people. They weren't giving signs on purpose. But when the horse tapped out the right answer, they showed something in their faces. Some smiled. The eyes of others lit up. Some sighed or clapped their hands.

The puzzle was solved. Hans was smart enough for a horse. He had not given right answers with human sense. He had done it with *horse sense*.

Can Ants Communicate?

by Dorothy Van Woerkam
illustrated by Dave Blanchette

For hundreds of years people have wondered if ants could communicate. They work so well together. They seem to follow a plan. They never get in each other's way. How did they do it? Do they communicate with one another?

Many years ago someone decided to try an experiment with the ants. First, a nail was driven into the ceiling of a room. A piece of string was tied to the nail. The other end of the string was tied round a pot of jam. The pot swayed slowly as it hung from the string.

Then one ant was put in the open pot of jam. Before long the ant made two discoveries. It found that it was alone in the pot, and that it was caught up in the air. The ant crawled down the outside of the pot. It ran round and round the bottom. Each time it circled the pot it seemed more frantic. No one could give the ant help. For the test to work, the ant had to find the way by itself.

After a very long while, the ant did. It crawled up the string. It walked across the ceiling. Down the wall it went. It ran round the edge of the room until it found the path to its home.

The seconds ticked away. Time passed. Then a half hour was gone. Still there was no sign of the ant. The test had failed. But perhaps not! All at once a large number of ants burst from the small hole in the wall where the first ant had gone. They did not waste a moment. They knew just where they were going.

They raced up the wall. At the ceiling they went straight to the nail. Then they marched down the string. Down they went, one at a time. Soon these ants reached the pot of jam. Just then another ant army came out of the hole in the wall.

One line of ants crawled down the string. Another line climbed up. This went on and on. Each ant could carry just a bit of jam, but there were many, many ants, and they worked very hard! Bit by bit they took all the jam from the pot to their home down below.

The ants had passed the test. The first ant had gone straight home to tell its friends about the jam. In some way the other ants got the message, and they knew where to go to get the jam. Clearly, ants can communicate.

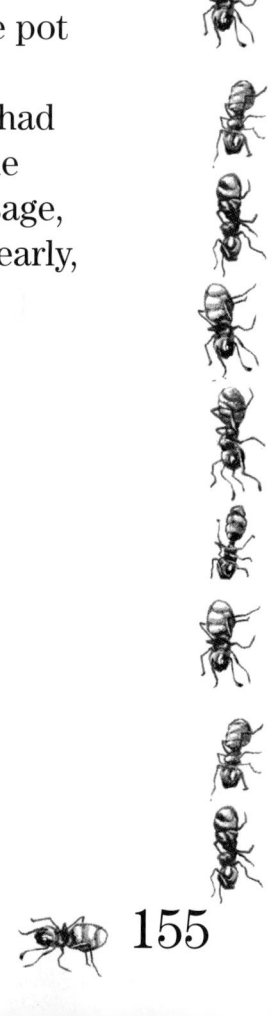

The Cave Paintings

by Theresa Bartlett

One day an anthropologist named Don Marcelino went into the Altamira cave near his home in Spain. He took his five-year-old daughter Maria with him.

Maria knew what her father was searching for in the cave. He was looking for tools that were thousands of years old.

Don Marcelino knew that people had found old tools in other caves. So he thought he might find some in this cave.

Don Marcelino had been digging for a long time when he found a stone tool.

"Maria!" he called. "Come and look!"

Maria looked at the tool. There was a picture carved on it.

"It's a picture of a horse," Maria said.

"Yes," Don Marcelino said, "it is a picture of a horse. But this horse isn't like our horses. There haven't been horses like this in Spain for thousands of years. The person who carved this horse must have lived here thousands of years ago."

Don Marcelino went on digging.

Maria watched him for a while. But then she grew bored. She went for a brief walk in the cave.

Suddenly, Maria exclaimed, "Papa! Papa! I see bulls!"

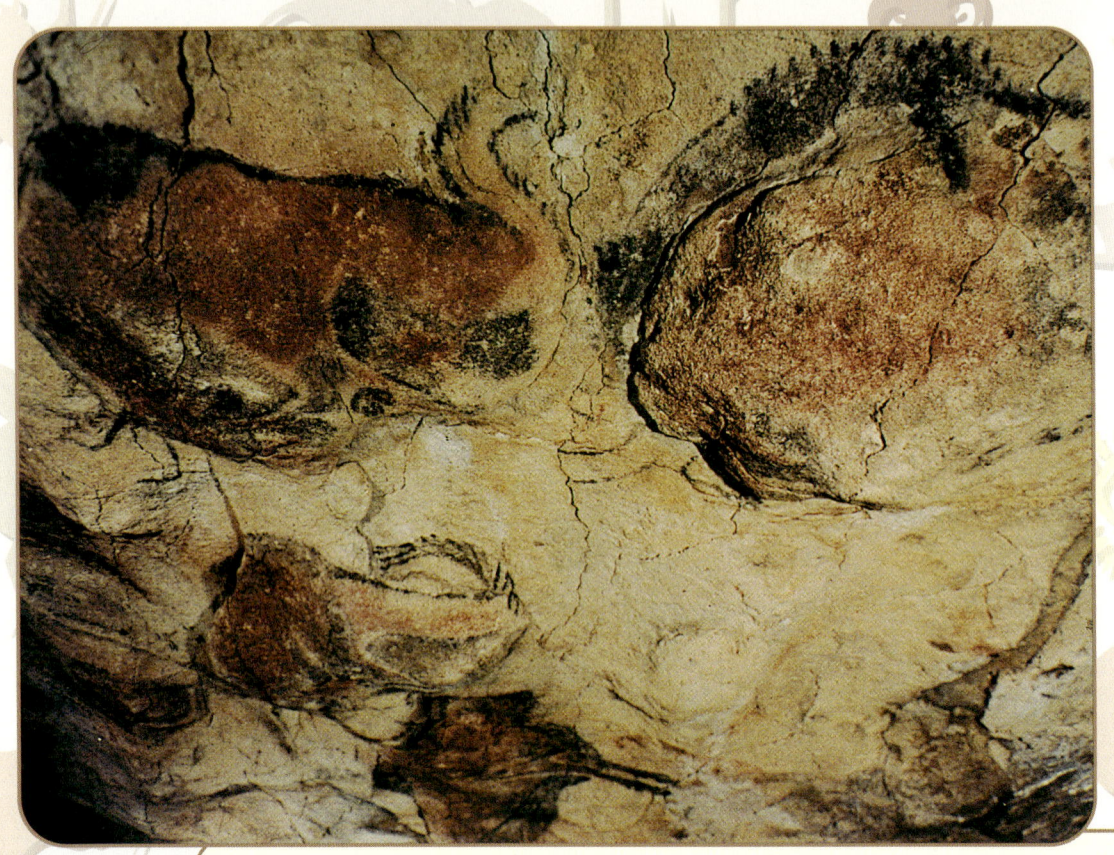

Don Marcelino went to Maria. The top of the cave was very low. So when Don Marcelino walked around in it, he had to keep his head down.

"I don't see any bulls," he said.

"There!" Maria pointed to the top of the cave.

Don Marcelino sat down on the floor. He had to sit down to see the top of the cave. When he sat down, he saw the bulls. They were red, and they seemed so real they almost seemed to be moving.

"Maria," said Don Marcelino, "you have made a great discovery! Just like the horses on the stone tool, these bulls are different from the bulls in Spain today. The painter must have lived when the toolmaker lived, thousands of years ago."

That night Don Marcelino wrote a letter to a friend who was a scientist. He told his friend about the cave paintings, and he asked him to come and see them.

His friend came as soon as he could. He was very excited when he saw the paintings.

"How wonderful!" he said. "People have found old pictures carved on tools before. But they've never found anything like this. No one knew before that the people of long ago could paint such lovely pictures."

Don Marcelino and his friend went deeper into the cave. There they found more paintings.

"Your daughter has made a great discovery," his friend said. "People from all over the world will want to see these paintings. This cave will be famous."

It was true. The Altamira cave has become famous. Thousands have gone to see the paintings, and from them they have learned much about the lives of early people. The people of long ago found a way to communicate with all who came after them.

Haiku: Fun to Read, Fun to Write

by Laura Joseph
illustrated by Beatriz Rodriguez

Since ancient times, people have used poetry as a means of communicating feelings and impressions. A special type of poem, called a *haiku*, is very popular in Japan.

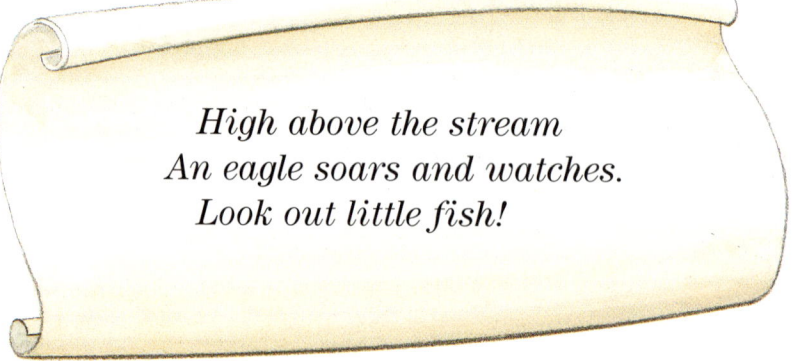

High above the stream
An eagle soars and watches.
Look out little fish!

This poem is a haiku. A haiku must say something about nature. The lines of a haiku do not rhyme. Try counting the syllables in each line. You should discover that the first and last lines have five syllables. The middle line has seven syllables. Here's another haiku.

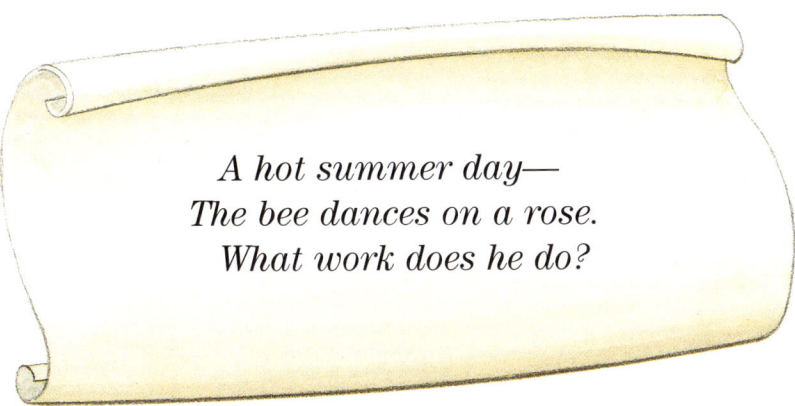

A hot summer day—
The bee dances on a rose.
What work does he do?

Like the first haiku, this one has seventeen syllables. It is also about nature. These verses don't tell long stories. They are like little pieces of time. They make you pay attention to just one little action or object.

In the 1600s, a Japanese man named Matsuo Munefusa wrote many poems like these. One day, one of Matsuo's students gave him a big basho tree. *Basho* is a Japanese word meaning "banana." The tree had huge leaves that tore apart in the wind. No bananas grew on the tree. The weather was too cold. Matsuo was very playful. "I love this tree," he said, "because it is useless—like me." After that, people called him *Basho*.

Before Basho's time, a haiku was just a funny little verse. People thought it didn't mean much. But Basho thought a haiku should be much more. He told people to "look very closely at ordinary things in nature." He told people to pretend to *be* those objects. Then they would know more about them. They would really understand them. Then Basho asked people what feelings they got from those objects. He told people to put those feelings into their haiku.

Basho wanted people to find new meaning in nature. He believed that a haiku should make them think in a different way. They should pursue a new feeling about an object—a blade of grass, for example.

*A blade of green grass
Bent as you skipped on the lawn,
Reaches for sunlight.*

A blade of grass must be very strong. People might step on it. They might even cut it with a lawn mower. But it keeps on growing—reaching for the sun. How would you feel if you were that blade of grass?

Think about the little scene this next haiku calls forth. What pictures can you see? What can you smell or taste? How does it make you feel?

*Snow covers the ground.
Alone, I eat my breakfast—
Hot toast and cold milk.*

Even ordinary things like breakfast can seem new. But remember, nature must always be included in a haiku. This haiku tells you it is a snowy morning.

Here's another scene. Is it familiar?

Above the houses
Filled with the smells of cooking
A full moon floating.

A haiku is fun to read or write. It can take you by surprise. It can make you see, think, or feel things in a new way. In a few words, a haiku can tell a wonderful story.

In the misty rain
The mountain hides its bare head.
How strange! Where is it?

UNIT 5

Reading Reflections

These questions can help you think about the stories you just read. After you write your responses, discuss them with a partner.

Focus on the Characters

- What personal qualities would help someone like Lisa in "How Lisa Learns to Talk" learn to communicate orally?
- Why do you think Mr. Easter wanted to teach Hans to count in "The Horse Who Could Count"?
- Compare and contrast Maria Marcelino, Don Marcelino, and Don Marcelino's friend in "The Cave Paintings."

Focus on the Stories

- Which two selections involved experiments to see if animals can communicate?
- Why was Maria Marcelino's discovery so important in "The Cave Paintings"?
- As explained in "Haiku: Fun to Read, Fun to Write," what makes a good haiku?

Communication

Focus on the Theme

- The theme of this unit is Communication. What different types of communication are discussed in this unit?
- What does the selection "Can Windmills Talk?" tell you about communication?
- After reading the stories in this unit, how important do you think communication is to you?

The Penobscot Hero

A Native American Folktale
retold by Martin Highbanks
illustrated by Fabricio Vanden Broeck

The Penobscot People living by the Penobscot River on the land now called Maine had a great mythical hero. His name was Gluska'be, and he was a trickster who used his magical talents to help his people. This is a tale of one of Gluska'be's innovative deeds that made life better for the Penobscot People.

Winter was long and cold where Gluska'be and his people lived.

Gluska'be said to his grandmother, "Winter cold is too long and brings misery to our people. I must bring Summer. Where does he live?"

"Summer lives in the South and is guarded day and night."

"I am going there. Make a pair of snowshoes. Then, cut hide strips and make me seven big balls from them."

She did as he asked, and he went away. Soon, he could not use his snowshoes, for it was too warm. So he hung them on a tall tree and left them there.

He walked on until he came to a wigwam where people were dancing.

"Why are you dancing?" he asked.

"Why are you asking?" they answered gruffly.

Gluska'be laughed and turned their noses upside down.

He watched the dancers make turns around a great bowl. Inside it was the yellow-golden jelly that was Summer.

Two young girls danced near him.

"Why are you dancing, little girls?" he asked.

They turned their backs and rejoined the dance without answering.

He patted them on their heads. Slowly they were transformed into toads and sat down. The other dancers ignored the amphibious pair and kept on turning.

"I must get Summer from them," Gluska'be said softly.

Without disrupting the dance, he made the wigwam dark, took the great bowl with Summer in it, and ran out.

As the wigwam became light again, the dancers saw that the bowl with Summer was gone.

"Summer has been taken by the stranger!" they cried, and ran out to search for him.

They became giant crows and flew in all directions. Soon, they saw Gluska'be and swooped down on him.

He put the ball of hide strips on his head. The crows took hold of it, thinking it was Gluska'be's head, but soon they saw that it was not. They flew back to him and swooped down, but again he had put a ball of hide strips on his head. The giant crows picked it off only to find again that it was not his head.

They did this five more times. Then, they became tired and did not follow him anymore.

Gluska'be ran until he came to the tree where his snowshoes were. He put them on and raced to the great Ice House where the giant Ice-Person sat all the time, breathing icy air into the land.

"What do you want, Gluska'be?" he asked.

"You must end blowing your ice-cold air all the time, for it makes people suffer."

"But they can look at the pretty ice I make," said the Ice-Person.

"Cold all the time brings suffering. I will end it."

"You are not strong enough," said the Ice-Person haughtily.

"No, but I brought one with me who is." Gluska'be put Summer before the great Ice-Person, who began to melt and drip.

"Take him away!" he roared. His nose was melting.

"It is too cold, and people suffer too much," said Gluska'be.

"Take him away!"

Ice-Person's great body began to melt. He grew smaller and smaller.

"Take . . . take . . ." He was all melted and could say no more.

Gluska'be was satisfied. "Now it won't be so cold and fierce. Summer, you stay here. When you are tired, go away so that Ice-Person can bring Winter back. But after a time, you must come back so people can have a rest from Ice-Person's winter cold."

And so it was.

Pearl Sunrise

by Nancy J. Nielsen

Pearl Sunrise is a Navajo. She lives in Albuquerque, New Mexico. There she makes beautiful multicolored Navajo cloth and blankets. She teaches others how to make them, too.

When Pearl was a little girl, she lived with her family in the country. Pearl's mother was quite a fine weaver. She taught Pearl how to spin wool into yarn and how to weave the yarn into beautiful cloth.

Pearl's parents were sheep herders. When Pearl was nine years old, she began herding sheep. She would take the sheep far up into the hills and watch them all day long. There she would sit and amuse herself by spinning wool into yarn.

Pearl and her brothers and sisters helped their parents in other ways, too. They chopped wood, they cared for the cattle, and they learned the Navajo ways from their parents and their grandfather and grandmother.

In those days, Navajo girls usually wore long skirts with high brown shoes. Pearl did not like to wear a long skirt when she herded sheep. So sometimes she wore her brother's jeans, but her parents did not like this.

One day, Pearl was sent away to school. She did not want to leave her family. None of the teachers were Navajo. They did not know anything about the ways of the Navajo. They were not bilingual. Pearl and the other pupils were allowed to speak only English instead of Navajo. Pearl felt the school was trying to change her too much.

When Pearl got back home from school, her father could see how much she had changed. She no longer wore her hair long as Navajo women do. She wore jeans all the time instead of Navajo skirts. Her father was very unhappy and wished that Pearl had not gone to the school.

In a trice, Pearl was living the Navajo way once more. She learned how to make Navajo baskets. She also learned more about weaving. She enjoyed being home again.

Pearl began to weave beautiful cloth and blankets. She colors her yarn by using wild plants and berries. As a Navajo, Pearl learned to respect nature. First, she asks Earth if it is all right to take the berries and plants. She tells Earth that she is taking them for her work. Then she is careful to take only as much as she needs.

Each of Pearl's blankets tells a story. Through her polychromatic blankets, Pearl tells others about herself and her people.

Over the decades she has worked, Pearl has won many prizes for her weaving. She likes to do her work because it makes her feel good. She is proud to be a Navajo.

Sequoya's New Alphabet

by Rob Howell
illustrated by Fabricio Vanden Broeck

As a Cherokee child in the late 1700s, Sequoya was fascinated by what his people called the "talking leaves." They were referring to printed books that people read and the sheets of paper that people wrote messages on. The Cherokees at that time did not have a written language.

The Job Begins

When Sequoya had grown up, he got the idea to create a special alphabet for his people so they could write their stories for all to read. But creating an alphabet for the Cherokee language was not that easy. At first, he tried to give every word its own written symbol. But he soon realized there were just too many words to do that. So instead, he created a symbol for each sound in the Cherokee language.

Sequoya began working on his alphabet in 1809. It was a huge job that he finished twelve years later in 1821. In the end, he had created symbols for 86 different sounds. But would the Cherokee people accept this new kind of communication, after relying all their lives only on the old method of speech?

Testing the Results

According to legend, Sequoya asked his daughter to model how well his alphabet worked. A panel of Cherokee chiefs privately told Sequoya what to write on paper. After Sequoya wrote it, his daughter read it aloud easily. The chiefs were fully convinced that the new alphabet was good.

Sequoya's alphabet was so simple that it could be learned in just a few days. Those who learned it first were soon able to teach it to others. Within just a few months, nearly all the Cherokees in that region were able to read and write using the new alphabet.

A Changed People

Sequoya's new alphabet allowed the Cherokees to record information about their own nation. They were also able to use the alphabet to publish books and newspapers in their own language. Through his hard work, Sequoya helped his people communicate with each other and preserve the wonderful stories that had been retold over the generations.

The Aztecs

by Walter Dubois

In 1519, a king named Moctezuma was the sole ruler of a large empire. He lived in the great city of Tenochtitlán. This mysterious city was on an island in the center of a lake. The people that lived there were called Aztecs. What happened to Tenochtitlán? Where are the Aztecs now?

The Aztecs lived in what is now called Mexico. Mexico City is built on the ruins of Tenochtitlán. The Aztecs' empire was conquered by Spanish soldiers. Although the Spaniards tried to wipe out the Aztec language and customs, you can still see many Aztec customs today. In fact, many modern Mexicans' ancestors were Aztecs.

Tenochtitlán was a large city with many people. Aztec children lived with their parents. Their grandmothers, grandfathers, aunts, and uncles often lived in the same home. These big families lived in adobe houses. These houses were made of bricks of dried mud and straw. You can still see adobe homes in Mexico today.

Since Tenochtitlán was an island, the Aztecs dug canals through the city. People could travel on these canals in canoes. They also built bridges to connect their city to the shore. In this way, people from other cities could come to their outdoor market. The Aztecs did not use money. Instead, they traded corn or beans for cloth and other precious things. Most cities in Mexico still have outdoor markets.

The Aztecs were good farmers. They grew corn, tomatoes, beans, cotton, and potatoes. Some people still farm the way the Aztecs did. The Aztecs also hunted for deer, rabbits, and ducks. The most common food was a thin corn pancake. Mexicans still eat this pancake. They call it a *tortilla*. You may have eaten one yourself!

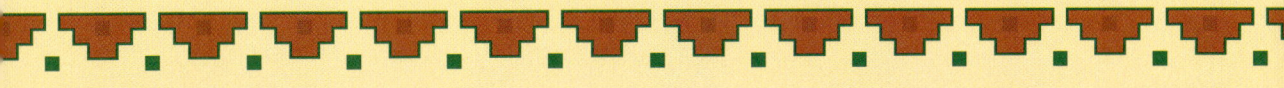

Some other foods also come from Aztec roots. The Aztecs invented a chocolate drink made from a special bean. We use this bean to make chocolate candy. The name for chocolate even comes from the Aztec language.

The Aztec way of life did not just disappear. We eat many Aztec foods. We still know and use some Aztec words. Although the Aztecs are gone, some of their customs still live on today.

Kiana's Discovery

by Sheri Cooper Sinykin
illustrated by Deborah White

"Kiana Braveheart?" the teacher read the name from the brown sack that she dangled in the air.

"That's mine!" Kiana sang out, jumping up to get her lunch. She joined some friends under a flowering fruit tree and began to eat.

Suddenly, two boys charged toward her out of the trees, pushing and laughing. Kiana held on to her sandwich and made a face.

"I'm king of the mountain!" one cried.

"No, Todd! I am!" said the other boy.

"What mountain?" Kiana said. "I don't see anything. Why don't you two go play somewhere else?"

"Just shows what you know," Todd said. "Come see for yourself."

Kiana followed them. Todd and the other boy raced on ahead, charging up a mound of earth.

"See?" Todd said. "What did I tell you?"

Kiana walked around the mound, looking at it from all sides. One thing was certain. This was no mountain. It had a strange shape, yet there was something familiar about it, too.

It made her think of the huge Indian mound shaped like a coiled snake that she and her mother and father had found some weeks ago peeking out of the snow. She remembered how they'd fixed special herbs and sprinkled them over the mound, and how they'd filled their hearts with loving words for the spirits of buried Indians now returned to earth.

A thrill swept through Kiana as she looked again at the strangely shaped mound. She knew exactly what she'd found. It was an Indian mound in the shape of a bear.

"Please!" she begged the boys. "Don't play on the mound." Then she explained why they shouldn't. The boys, excited by her discovery, ran back to tell the teachers.

Kiana breathed in the silence and whispered a word of thanks. Then she hurried about the forest, collecting barks and plants to make her own special herbs.

Standing over the mound, her head bowed, Kiana opened her heart and let her feelings wash through. She knew that words—the right words—would come soon. She'd share her respect for the Indians who lived before her and for the earth where she—and they—lived now.

And as surely as her name meant "Spirit Protector," she knew she'd need no pen, no paper, to speak the words and get them right.

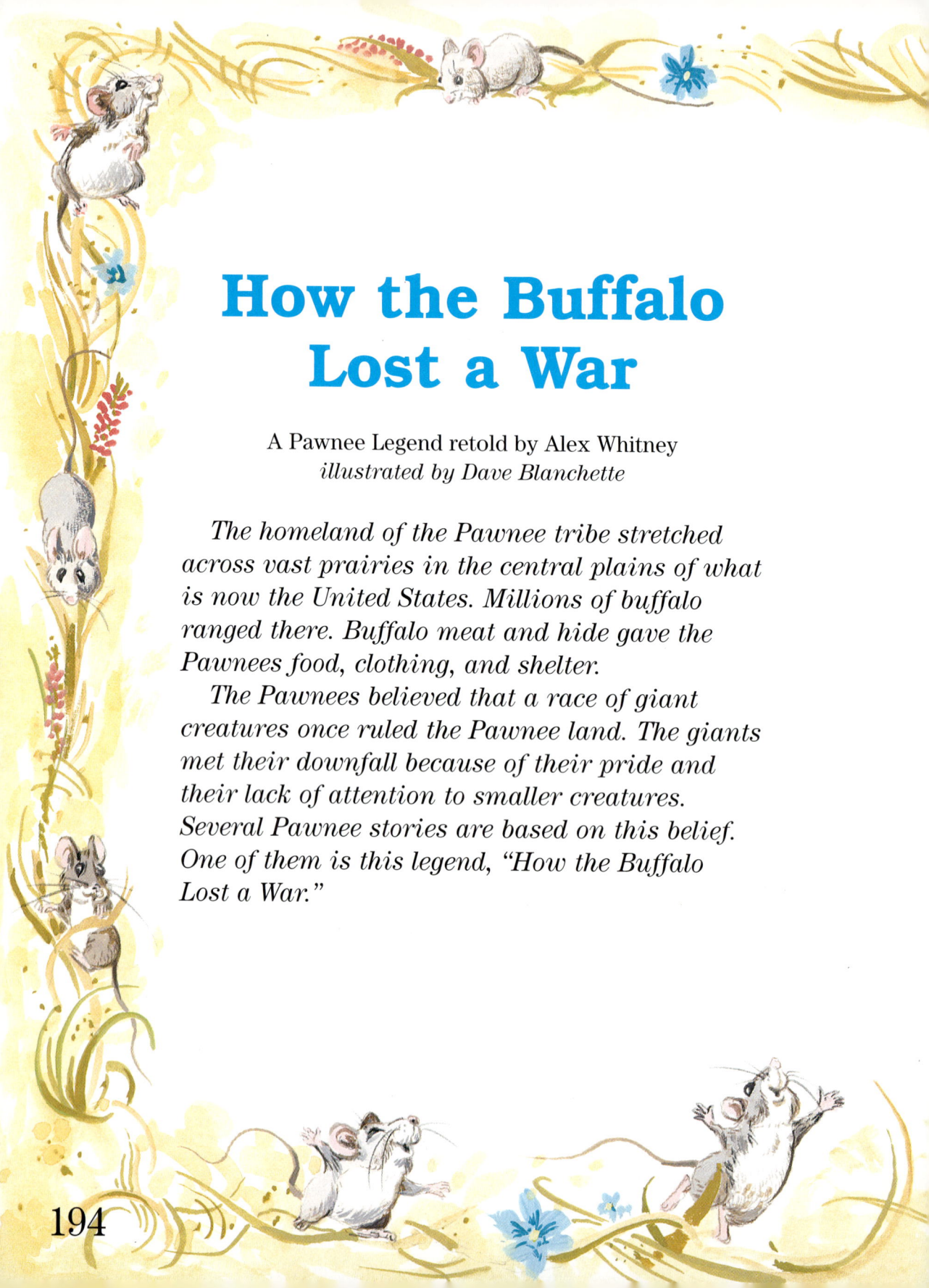

How the Buffalo Lost a War

A Pawnee Legend retold by Alex Whitney
illustrated by Dave Blanchette

The homeland of the Pawnee tribe stretched across vast prairies in the central plains of what is now the United States. Millions of buffalo ranged there. Buffalo meat and hide gave the Pawnees food, clothing, and shelter.

The Pawnees believed that a race of giant creatures once ruled the Pawnee land. The giants met their downfall because of their pride and their lack of attention to smaller creatures. Several Pawnee stories are based on this belief. One of them is this legend, "How the Buffalo Lost a War."

One day near the beginning of winter, the field mouse stepped out of her nest of dried yellow grass in the small prairie meadow. She sniffed the crisp, tangy air. Soon, she knew, the north wind would sweep the prairie with his frost-tipped wings. It was time, she thought, to gather her food, for there would be long, cold days and nights ahead.

While the mouse searched busily for wild beans in the tall grass, a buffalo bull as large as a giant came into the meadow to graze. The sight of the huge, shaggy beast alarmed the little mouse. She was afraid he would eat most of the grass, and he might mow down the rest with his hooves and his rough tongue. "There'll be no place left in which to hide," said the mouse to herself as she hurried towards the newcomer.

"Greetings!" said the mouse to the buffalo. "Welcome to the meadow. But do save a small patch of it for me, won't you?"

The buffalo, munching on a mouthful of grass, did not look at her.

The mouse was about to repeat her plea in a louder tone of voice when she saw the huge beast step on her nest of dried grass.

"Ho, buffalo!" squeaked the mouse, her whiskers bristling. "Thanks to your big hoof, you've destroyed my only shelter from the north wind! Leave this meadow at once. If you don't, I'll challenge you to a war!"

The buffalo looked down with scorn at the mouse. "Don't be foolish, little one!" he snorted. "You're far too small to wage war with me!"

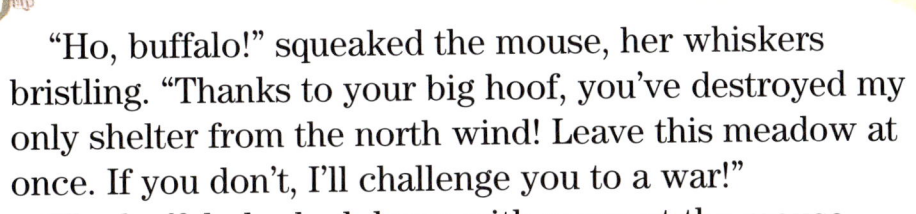

A moment later, the buffalo felt a tickle inside his right ear. He shook his head from side to side and twitched his ears back and forth. But the tickly feeling only increased. Flinging his tail in the air, he ran straight ahead. Then he ran in circles. At last he stopped abruptly. The mouse jumped out of his ear and to the ground.

The buffalo stared with surprise at the mouse. "Ho! So you're the one who's been tickling me!" he exclaimed angrily. "I'll show you what happens to little ones who have no respect for mighty giants!" And, lowering his huge head, the big beast charged at the tiny mouse. But she quickly sprang on top of the beast's head.

Once more the buffalo felt a maddening tickle. This time it was inside his left ear. Crazed with rage, he pawed the air with his front hooves. He tore up the grass with his sharp horns. Then he wheeled about and galloped out of the meadow. He had become a whirling and bellowing tornado. In a cloud of dust, he plunged recklessly down a rocky hillside. At last he stopped in the valley below. The mouse leaped out of his ear and to the ground. Then her enemy turned and ran away.

"Do you still claim I'm too small to wage war with you, O mighty giant?" the mouse yelled after him.

She listened for his reply. But all she heard was the faint pounding of hooves in the distance.

UNIT 6

Reading Reflections

These questions can help you think about the stories you just read. After you write your responses, discuss them with a partner.

Focus on the Characters

- Compare Pearl Sunrise as a schoolgirl and as an adult.
- Compare and contrast the mouse and the buffalo in "How the Buffalo Lost a War."
- Do you think Gluska'be is a hero or a villain? Explain your answer.

Focus on the Stories

- What effect did Sequoya have on the Cherokee Nation?
- Pearl Sunrise did not reject the traditions of the Navajo people. Name another story in this unit where a girl continued on with the traditions of her people.
- What Aztec customs still live on today?

Native Americans

Focus on the Theme

- The tribes presented in this unit lived in various parts of the United States and Mexico. They lived in different types of houses and had different languages. Despite their differences, what was one quality that they shared?
- What have you learned about Native Americans through reading the selections in this unit?
- It is important for Native Americans to teach their traditions to their children so that their customs will not disappear. What is a tradition in your family that is passed on or that you hope will continue?

Glossary

Pronunciation Key

a as in **a**t	**o** as in **o**x	**ou** as in **ou**t	**ch** as in **ch**air
ā as in l**a**te	**ō** as in r**o**se	**u** as in **u**p	**hw** as in **wh**ich
â as in c**a**re	**ô** as in b**ou**ght and r**a**w	**ū** as in **u**se	**ng** as in ri**ng**
ä as in f**a**ther		**ûr** as in t**ur**n; g**er**m, l**ear**n, f**ir**m, w**or**k	**sh** as in **sh**op
e as in s**e**t	**oi** as in c**oi**n		**th** as in **th**in
ē as in m**e**	**o͝o** as in b**oo**k	**ə** as in **a**bout, chick**e**n, penc**i**l, cann**o**n, circ**u**s	**t͟h** as in **th**ere
i as in **i**t	**o͞o** as in t**oo**		**zh** as in trea**s**ure
ī as in k**i**te	**or** as in f**or**m		

The mark (´) is placed after a syllable with a heavy accent, as in chicken (chik´ən).

The mark (ˈ) after a syllable shows a lighter accent, as in disappear (dis´ ə pēr´).

A

accident (ak´ si dənt) *n.* Something that happens and is not expected.

accomplished (ə kom´ plisht) *v.* Past tense of **accomplish**: To succeed in completing.

amazement (ə māz´ mənt) *n.* Overwhelming wonder or surprise.

amphibious (am fib´ ē əs) *adj.* Capable of living both on land and in water, such as a toad.

ancestors (an´ ses tûrz) *n.* Plural form of **ancestor**: Someone from whom one is descended.

anthropologist (an´ thrə pol´ ə jist) *n.* A student of or expert in the physical, cultural, and social development of humans.

applauding (ə plôd´ ing) A form of the verb **applaud**: To show approval or enjoyment by clapping the hands.

argue (är´ gū) *v.* To have a discussion and disagree.

audience (ô´ dē əns) *n.* A group of people gathered to hear or see something, such as a concert.

autocorrection (ô´ tō kə rek´ shən) *n.* A self-made change to an error.

B

bargain (bär´ gin) *n.* Something bought or offered at a low price.

bellowing (bel´ ō ing) *adj.* Loud and deep in sound.

bilingual (bī ling´ gwəl) *adj.* Able to speak two languages with equal or nearly equal skill and ease.

202

Glossary

blizzards

blizzards (bliz´ ûrdz) *n.* Plural form of **blizzard:** A severe, heavy snowstorm with strong winds.

blots (blots) A form of the verb **blot:** To cover up completely.

bow (bou) *n.* The forward end of a boat.

boycotted (boi´ kot id) *v.* Past tense of **boycott:** To refuse to do business or have contact with another person, group, business, or government.

braided (brā´ did) *adj.* Twisted together.

brief (brēf) *adj.* Short in time.

budge (buj) *v.* To move slightly or give way.

buoys (bōō´ ēz) *n.* Plural form of **buoy:** An anchored floating device used to warn ships about hazards.

burst (bûrst) *v.* To come in or appear suddenly.

C

carved (kärvd) *v.* Past tense of **carve:** To decorate by cutting figures or designs.

clutch (kluch) *v.* To hold firmly.

coaxed (kōkst) *v.* Past tense of **coax:** To persuade through flattery, pleasant manner, or gifts.

coiled (koild) A form of the verb **coil:** To wind tightly.

decorated

cold front (kōld´ frunt´) *n.* The forward edge of a mass of cold air moving into an area of warmer air.

collapsed (kə lapsd´) *v.* Past tense of **collapse:** To fall in or cave in.

conquered (kong´ kûrd) A form of the verb **conquer:** To defeat.

considered (kən sid´ ûrd) *v.* Past tense of **consider:** To think carefully about.

constructing (kən strukt´ ing) A form of the verb **construct:** To put together; build.

coward (kou´ ûrd) *n.* Someone who lacks courage or is easily frightened.

customer (kus´ tə mûr) *n.* Someone who shops or buys.

customs (kus´ təmz) *n.* Plural form of **custom:** A common practice.

D

Damascus (də mas´ kəs) *n.* The capital and largest city of Syria, a nation in the Middle East.

dangled (dang´ gəld) *v.* Past tense of **dangle:** To hang down loosely.

dashed (dashd) *v.* Past tense of **dash:** To rush.

decipher (di sī´ fûr) *v.* To figure out the meaning of something difficult to understand.

decorated (dek´ ə rā´ ted) *v.* Past tense of **decorate:** To make more beautiful.

Glossary

delivered (di liv´ ûrd) A form of the verb **deliver:** To take to a particular place or person.

disappointed (dis´ ə poin´ ted) A form of the verb **disappoint:** To frustrate; let down.

downfall (doun´ fôl´) *n.* A fall from power and prosperity.

drifted (drif´ təd) *v.* Past tense of **drift:** To be moved along by currents of water.

E

employment (em ploi´ mənt) *adj.* Dealing with job opportunities.

entangled (en tang´ gəld) *v.* Past tense of **entangle:** To catch in a net.

excitement (ek sīt´ mənt) *n.* A state of high emotions.

exclaimed (ek sklāmd´) *v.* Past tense of **exclaim:** To speak or cry out suddenly.

exhausted (eg zôs´ ted) *adj.* Extremely weak and tired.

experimented (ek sper´ ə mən ted) *v.* Past tense of **experiment:** To test or try out an idea.

F

fascinated (fas´ ə nā´ ted) A form of the verb **fascinate:** To attract and hold interest.

flinging (fling´ ing) A form of the verb **fling:** To toss with force.

frantic (fran´ tik) *adj.* Wildly excited by worry, grief, fear, or anger.

frigid (frij´ id) *adj.* Very cold.

G

gobbled (gob´ əld) *v.* Past tense of **gobble:** To eat quickly and greedily.

H

haughtily (hô´ tə lē) *adv.* With much pride in oneself and looking down on others.

hazardous (haz´ ûr dəs) *adj.* Risky.

hemisphere (he´ mə sfēr) *n.* One half of the earth, as divided by the equator or the Greenwich meridian.

horizon (hə rī´ zən) *n.* The line where the sky seems to meet with the land or sea.

horse sense (hors´ sens´) *n.* Practical common sense.

hovered (huv´ ûrd) *v.* Past tense of **hover:** To linger or remain nearby.

I

illogical (i loj´ i kəl) *adj.* Showing a lack of good sense or reasoning.

improbable (im prob´ ə bəl) *adj.* Unlikely.

independent (in´ di pen´ dənt) *adj.* Self-supporting.

Glossary

injuries

injuries (in´ jə rēz) *n.* Plural form of **injury:** Damage done to a person or thing.

innovative (in´ ə vā´ tiv) *adj.* New and fresh.

inventions (in ven´ chənz) *n.* Plural form of **invention:** A newly created object or process.

involved (in volvd´) A form of the verb **involve:** To occupy completely; absorb.

J

jerked (jûrkd) *v.* Past tense of **jerk:** To give a sudden sharp pull.

junction (jungk´ shən) *n.* A place where two or more things join or meet.

L

lentils (len´ təlz) *n.* Plural form of **lentil:** The seed of a plant related to the pea that is cooked and eaten as a vegetable.

liberate (lib´ ə rāt) *v.* To set free; release.

life preservers (līf´ pri zûrv´ ûrz) *n.* Plural form of **life preserver:** A flotation device.

linen (lin´ ən) *adj.* Made of a strong cloth that is similar to cotton.

mussed

lipread (lip´ rēd) *v.* To understand what someone is saying by watching the movements of the lips, used especially by people who are hearing impaired.

M

memorized (mem´ə rīzd´) A form of the verb **memorize:** To commit to memory; learn by heart.

merchants (mûr´ chəntz) *n.* Plural form of **merchant:** Someone whose business is selling things.

mesh (mesh) *adj.* Having open spaces between interlocking material, such as a net.

microscopic (mī´ krə skop´ ik) *adj.* Too small to be seen with the naked eye.

migrant (mī´ grənt) *n.* Someone who moves from one country or region to another in order to settle there.

miller (mil´ ur) *n.* Someone who owns or operates a mill for grinding grain.

mission (mish´ ən) *n.* A goal or task.

models (mod´ əlz) *n.* Plural form of **model:** A design or type.

multicolored (mul´ ti kul´ urd) *adj.* Of many or various colors.

murmurs (mûr´ mûrz) *n.* Plural form of **murmur:** A low, continuous sound.

mussed (must) *v.* Past tense of **muss:** To make untidy.

205

Glossary

N

nag (nag) *v.* To annoy with repeated requests to do something.

nervous (nûr´ vəs) *adj.* Tense and restless.

nobleman (nō´ bəl mən) *n.* A man of noble birth, rank, or title.

O

observers (əb zûrv´ ûrz) *n.* Plural form of **observer:** Someone who watches something.

offered (ô´ fûrd) *v.* Past tense of **offer:** To propose for consideration.

ordinary (or´ də nâr´ ē) *adj.* Usual or regular.

origin (or´ i jin) *n.* The source of something.

outfoxed (out´ fokst´) *v.* Past tense of **outfox:** To outsmart.

P

perform (pûr form´) *v.* To present a play, musical, or other entertainment to the public.

permission (pûr mish´ ən) *n.* Consent to do something.

phonograph (fô´ nə graf´) *n.* A device that reproduces sounds recorded on a disk of plastic or other material.

polychromatic (pol´ ē krō mat´ ik) *adj.* Of many or various colors.

preserve (pri zûrv´) *v.* To maintain or keep.

pretend (pri tend´) *v.* To give a false appearance of.

promises (prom´ is ez) *n.* Plural form of **promise:** A pledge to do or not do something.

promotes (prə mōtz´) A form of the verb **promote:** To help or contribute to something.

pulp (pulp) *n.* Any soft, moist, formless mass used in making paper.

pursue (pûr soo´) *v.* To seek for.

R

recovered (ri kuv´ ûrd) A form of the verb **recover:** To regain.

relying (ri lī´ ing) A form of the verb **rely:** To depend on.

retired (ri tīrd´) *v.* Past tense of **retire:** To finish one's professional career.

rogue wave (rōg´ wāv´) *n.* An especially large and dangerous wave.

S

scales (skālz) *n.* The plural form of **scale:** A series of tones that go up and down in pitch according to fixed intervals.

scorn (skorn) *n.* A feeling of contempt for someone or something.

scrambled

scrambled (skram´ bəld) *v.* Past tense of **scramble:** To go quickly or frantically.

segregation (seg´ ri gā´ shən) *n.* Keeping different races of people apart from each other.

snowshoes (snō´ sho͞oz´) *n.* Plural form of **snowshoe:** A light wooden frame strung with a webbing of rawhide or other material, fastened to the foot for walking over deep snow without sinking in.

stable (stā´ bəl) *n.* A building where horses and cattle are kept and fed.

stalls (stôlz) *n.* Plural form of **stall:** A booth or counter for setting up products for sale.

strained (strānd) *v.* Past tense of **strain:** To injure or weaken by excessive stretching.

swayed (swād) *v.* Past tense of **sway:** To move or swing back and forth or from side to side.

syllables (sil´ ə bəlz) *n.* Plural form of **syllable:** A words or word part pronounced with a single uninterrupted voice sounding.

T

tangy (tang´ ē) *adj.* Sharp in taste, flavor, or odor.

thoughtfully (thôt´ fəl lē) *adv.* With careful attention or consideration.

thrill (thril) *n.* An exciting feeling.

weavers

tins (tinz) *n.* Plural form of **tin:** A tin container, such as a food can.

transformed (trans formd´) A form of the verb **transform:** To change in shape, form, or appearance.

trice (trīs) *n.* An instant.

trick (trik) *v.* To deceive or cheat.

U

ultracold (ul´ trə kōld´) *n.* Extreme cold.

urged (ûrjd) *v.* Past tense of **urge:** To suggest forcefully.

V

vibration (vī brā´ shən) *n.* A shaking or quivering movement.

W

weavers (wē´ vûrz) *n.* Plural form of **weaver:** Someone who makes products by lacing together materials.